The God
That Limps

Norton/Worldwatch Books

Lester R. Brown: *The Twenty-Ninth Day: Accommodating Human Needs and Numbers to the Earth's Resources*

Lester R. Brown: *Building a Sustainable Society*

Lester R. Brown, Christopher Flavin, and Colin Norman: *Running on Empty: The Future of the Automobile in an Oil Short World*

Erik P. Eckholm: *Losing Ground: Environmental Stress and World Food Prospects*

Erik P. Eckholm: *The Picture of Health: Environmental Sources of Disease*

Denis Hayes: *Rays of Hope: The Transition to a Post-Petroleum World*

Kathleen Newland: *The Sisterhood of Man*

Colin Norman: *The God That Limps: Science and Technology in the Eighties*

Bruce Stokes: *Helping Ourselves: Local Solutions to Global Problems*

The God That Limps

Science and Technology
in the Eighties

Colin Norman

A Worldwatch Institute Book

W. W. Norton & Company
New York   London

Copyright © 1981 by Worldwatch Institute

Published simultaneously in Canada by George J. McLeod Limited, Toronto.

Printed in the United States of America

All Rights Reserved

First Edition

Library of Congress Cataloging in Publication Data
Norman, Colin, 1946–
   The God that limps.   Includes index.
    1. Technology—Social aspects. I. Title.
T14.5.N67 1981 306'.4 81–38328
ISBN 0–393–01504–1 AACR2

W. W. Norton & Company, Inc. 500 Fifth Avenue, New York, N.Y. 10110

W. W. Norton & Company Ltd. 25 New Street Square, London EC4A 3NT

1 2 3 4 5 6 7 8 9 0

To my parents, Jim and Marjorie Norman

Contents

Preface

Science and technology stand at the center of many of the critical issues facing society in the final two decades of the twentieth century. The arms race, the energy crisis, the problems of producing sufficient food, shelter, and material resources for a world population that will swell to 6 billion by the year 2000—all have technological dimensions. Small wonder, therefore, that science and technology occupy a prominent position in the hopes and fears of many people.

This book is an attempt to shed light on some of the relationships between technological change and society. I have looked at the role of technology in a global economy that has undergone profound—and probably irreversible—changes in the past decade or so, and I have explored the social, political, and economic forces that shape the processes of technological change. I make no claims of comprehensiveness, and this book is certainly not an attempt to survey the world's problems and suggest technological solutions for them. Rather, it is intended to show how political, social, and technological forces interact, and why reforms will be needed in all these areas if the problems confronting global society are to be resolved.

The United Nations Environment Programme and Worldwatch Institute jointly supported the research and writing that went into this book, and I am grateful to them for this support. Worldwatch Institute President Lester R. Brown originally suggested the idea of a book on technology, and his enthusiasm and encouragement throughout the project were invaluable.

The entire manuscript was reviewed by Lester Brown, Erik Eckholm, Christopher Flavin, Daniel Greenberg, Kathleen Newland, Pamela Shaw, Nigel Smith, Linda Starke, Bruce Stokes, Ann Thrupp, and Nicholas Wade. It benefited greatly from their critical insights.

Some of the ideas and analysis in this book are drawn from Worldwatch Papers I have written on issues connected with science and technology. Scores of people helped me in preparing those papers, and I would like to thank in particular David Dickson, Robert Fuller, Denis Hayes, Nicholas Jequier, Daniel Greenberg, Colin Hines, Ted Owens, Arthur Robinson, Nicholas Wade, and Charles Weiss, all of whom put aside their work to review early drafts. I am doubly indebted to Nicholas Wade for suggesting the title for the book.

Preparing a manuscript under tight deadlines is always an arduous process, but it was made considerably easier by Blondeen Gravely's impressive speed and efficiency in typing successive drafts. Elizabeth Arnault and Oretta Tarkhani chipped in with welcome assistance when needed, and Macinda Byrd helped greatly in collecting research materials.

John Donahue brought his editing skills to bear on the manuscript at short notice, and provided many valuable suggestions for improving not only the style but the logic as well. Writing a book places many demands on family and friends. I am indebted, as always, to Anne Norman for providing much-needed support and encouragement over many long months.

COLIN NORMAN

Worldwatch Institute
1776 Massachusetts Avenue, NW
Washington, D. C. 20036

The God
That Limps

1

The God
That Limps

Hephaestus, the Greek god of fire and metalworking, had a pronounced limp. Entrusted with the development and maintenance of many key technologies, Hephaestus was responsible for keeping society running smoothly and perfectly. Yet he was, ironically, the only imperfect member of the pantheon of classical gods. This ancient irony is compounded by current attitudes toward Hephaestus's crafts. Technology is the focus of much public homage, for it is often seen as the chief hope for solving the myriad problems facing society—a hope embodied in the oft-heard lament, "If they can put a man on the moon, why can't they . . . ?" Yet, at the same time, many of the ills of the modern world, from pollution to the threat of nuclear Armageddon, are frequently blamed on technological developments. As in Hephaestus himself, the power and versatility of technology are often marred by crippling defects.

There is, consequently, a good deal of ambivalence and uncertainty about technology and its role in society. The past decade has witnessed an intense and at times acrimonious debate about the nature and direction of technological developments. No longer are the fruits of technology received with unquestioning faith. Instead, battle lines have formed around many prominent technological ventures and the foundations of technological society have come under intense attack from a variety of critics.

This debate ebbed and flowed during the seventies, as a series of shocks ran through the global economy and as serious social problems surfaced in virtually every country. As these economic and social problems deepened, it gradually became clear that fundamental changes would be needed in the coming years as the world moves from an era of rapid economic growth and relatively abundant energy and material resources into a more uncertain period. Technological change has become urgent in many areas. It is thus not surprising that an intense debate has erupted over the contribution of technology both to the problems facing the world and to their potential resolution.

The growing doubts about the nature and direction of technological change are a far cry from the technological optimism that reigned in the fifties and early sixties. In those heady days, technology seemed to hold the key to a prosperous new world. The global economy was booming, humans were making their first tentative ventures into space, the Green Revolution seemed to promise a solution to the world food problem, and nuclear power was being proclaimed as a source of cheap, clean energy. It was a period when, as former U.S. Secretary of the Interior Stewart Udall has aptly put it, "there were no problems, only solutions" and when misgivings about technological developments could easily be brushed aside.[1]

There can be little real doubt that the steady stream of innovations produced in the past few decades has brought immense benefit to society. By virtually every measure, people are better clothed, housed, educated, and fed than they were a generation or so ago. New medical knowledge has led to the control of a host of infectious diseases, transportation and communications technologies have shrunk the planet, new agricultural and industrial processes have boosted productivity to unprecedented heights, and a wealth of new scientific findings have immeasurably enriched human culture. The Good Old Days, when disease, hunger, and backbreaking toil were everyday experiences, seem good only when viewed through the distorting lens of nostalgia.

But the benefits of these technological advances are at least partially offset by serious social and environmental costs, among which pollution, energy shortages, and growing dependence on nonrenewable resources are the most obvious. Moreover, technological skills have proven impotent in the face of such problems as urban decay, poverty, unemployment, racial strife, and disintegrating family structures. Indeed, many aspects of technological change have aggravated such problems.

In poor countries, too, the benefits of new technologies have been counterbalanced by heavy social costs. In the postwar years, when many former colonies achieved political independence, the accepted path to prosperity lay in raising economic growth rates as swiftly as possible. The transformation of agriculture and industry by technologies imported from the industrial countries was widely regarded as the open sesame to "rich-country" status. It has become clear, however, that these policies have brought little benefit to many of the world's poorest people: while economic growth rates have increased as expected in many developing countries, poverty, underemployment, and their attendant miseries have also increased. The Green Revolution has raised grain yields, for example, but malnutrition is still a fact of life and death for hundreds of millions of people—a grim reminder that technical fixes alone cannot solve complex social problems.

These tangible social and environmental costs explain some of the current feelings of ambivalence about modern technology. But there are other, deeper concerns. Among them is the widespread and deep-seated feeling that technology is out of control, that technological developments have a momentum of their own that is difficult, if not impossible, for individuals to influence. Former British Prime Minister Harold Wilson summed up this feeling in a speech in 1973, when he complained that technology is "running over people's lives." Ironically, a decade earlier, Wilson had led the Labour Party to victory with a campaign pledge to forge Britain's prosperity in the "white heat of technological revolution." So much for the technological optimism of the early sixties.[2]

The notion that technology is out of control has diverse roots. It stems in part from the very complexity of industrial society, in which most people are consigned to play relatively small roles in large economic organizations. The centralization of decision making in governments and giant corporations has deprived individuals of a real role in shaping policies that affect their lives—not only in the realm of technology, but in other areas as well. Beyond that, however, there is the inescapable fact that most technologies that intimately affect everyday life, from power plants to automobiles, are highly complex. Consequently, many people find their lives shaped by technologies that they do not understand and over which they have little control.

Government bureaucracies and large corporations account for most of the global expenditures on research and development, and they have the resources to take innovations from the laboratory bench through the testing stage and into widespread use. They are thus the prime actors in the development and application of new technologies. Public influence over this process is exercised chiefly through purchasing power in the marketplace—which is itself shaped by the advertising budgets of the industries that develop new technologies—and through political pressures in the halls of government. Usually, however, public influence is limited to attempts to curb the use of technologies that are already well along the path to development, such as nuclear power or supersonic transportation; there is little opportunity for individuals to have much impact on the processes that lead to the generation of new technologies.

Developing countries, moreover, are in an especially weak position to influence the direction of technological change, though they are fundamentally affected by it. Because they have little technological capacity of their own, most developing countries import technologies for their industrial and agricultural development, paying large sums of money for the technologies they acquire and becoming technologically dependent on the industrial countries. And, since those technologies are developed in the economic and cultural climate of the industrial world, they are not always well suited to the Third World's most pressing needs.

The technological revolution of the past few decades thus seems like a Faustian bargain to many people—economic and material progress bought at the expense of growing dependence on nonrenewable resources, of environmental degradation, and of loss of control over many aspects of everyday life. And the terms of the bargain seem to be quickly deteriorating as the world enters the final two decades of the twentieth century.

Although a schizophrenic mix of hope and concern characterizes public attitudes toward technology, there is little general understanding of how new technology is developed and applied. Yet the forces that shape the development of technology are key elements in determining the structure of society, for technology is so deeply embedded in virtually every aspect of life that technological changes and social changes often go hand-in-hand.

There is a widespread, if subconscious, belief that technological change is driven chiefly by its own momentum; advances in knowledge and technical understanding inevitably lead to the production and application of new technology which then causes changes in society. This notion lies behind such well-worn phrases as "the march of technology" and, as Langdon Winner has pointed out in his book, *Autonomous Technology*, it pervades much writing on technology and undergirds fears that technology is out of control.[3]

Technological development, according to this view, is an evolutionary process, not unlike biological evolution. We even speak of new "generations" of computers, automobiles, and other high-technology goods as if they were biological descendants of earlier models, and key technical developments are often regarded as the progenitors of a whole range of subsequent innovations. Closely linked to this view is the idea that social changes are technologically determined: new technologies, introduced into society, change the way society functions. Society, in other words, is largely a product of its technology. This concept lies unstated behind such terms as the Bronze Age, the Machine Age, and the Computer Age.

Thus, for example, the rise of cities in ancient Sumeria is often explained by the introduction of agricultural technologies that raised the production of food to a level that could support large numbers of people living away from the land. The harnessing of steam power has been described as giving birth to the machines of the Industrial Revolution. And, more recently, popular writers such as Alvin Toffler have portrayed a society shaped by technologies that flow in an endless stream from the world's laboratories. "Technology," asserts Toffler, is a "great, growling engine of change."[4]

These views of technology and social change provide a useful perspective on technology and society, and they offer a seductively simple explanation for complex social and political events. But they also raise some difficult questions, and they certainly cannot explain many aspects of technological development. If technology evolves largely according to its own dynamics, bringing social changes in its wake, why, for example, did the Industrial Revolution not take place in Ancient Greece, when the principles of steam power were first discovered? Why did other scientifically advanced civilizations not develop manufacturing technologies? And why are some technologies pursued while other, equally attractive technologies are neglected?

The answer to such questions is buried in the very concept of evolution. Technological evolution, like biological evolution, responds to a variety of forces. Biological evolution is driven by environmental pressures that favor the survivability of some species over others—insects resistant to an insecticide will swiftly predominate in a sprayed area, for example—and the key to the development of living things can be found only by looking at them in relation to their environment. Similarly, the key to technological development lies in the environment in which technological change takes place—in this case, the social, economic, political, and physical environment.

Corporations dominate the development of new technology in the western industrial countries and Japan, and commercial forces thus constitute a prominent part of the environment in which technological change takes place. They provide a powerful thrust that guides both the pace and direction of much technological development. The corporate system has been enormously productive in generating new technologies. The economic incentives to innovate—and the economic costs of not doing so in a competitive environment—have made corporations "highly efficient in exploring technological possibilities for new consumer products and devices that can be marketed and sold at a profit," notes Emmanuel Mesthene, former head of Harvard University's Program on Science and Society.[5]

Economic forces in general help explain many aspects of technological development. Corporations are interested in developing and applying technologies that will reduce the costs of production, capture a larger share of the market, raise the productivity of their workers, and otherwise contribute to the bottom line on their profit and loss statements. Similar, though less obvious, pressures also guide technological development in the centrally-planned industrial countries, where planning targets and a variety of incentives seek to raise productivity and to push down the costs of production. Thus, in an era when oil and gas were sold for next to nothing and the price of many materials was low and even declining, economic considerations led to the proliferation of technologies profligate in their use of energy and materials. Similarly, economic forces provide one reason why production processes have become increasingly capital-intensive and labor-saving in a period when capital has been relatively cheap and labor relatively expensive in the industrial world. And the economic advantages of producing goods in large quantities help explain why production processes, from power plants to automobile assembly lines, have become increasingly centralized and larger in scale.

Although economic forces clearly play a prominent role in shaping technological development, there is a vast amount of innovation for which they cannot account. Weapons, space vehicles, law enforcement technologies, health care systems, and education techniques are not developed primarily for their economic payoff. Nor are such activities as astronomy, high energy physics, and molecular biology supported simply because they offer a promising rate of financial return. Indeed, if economic forces alone were sufficient to drive technological development, corporations could be expected to carry out all the necessary innovation, and the role of governments could be limited to setting the correct economic and regulatory environment—or, according to the free marketeers, governments should simply get out of the way. In reality, every government has a direct stake in technological development. Government agencies fund a large fraction of national research and development efforts, they provide a major thrust to the development of new technologies through their purchasing programs, and they underwrite the costs of educating and training scientists and engineers.

Overt political and social pressures thus shape a good deal of technological development, providing a driving force that extends well beyond strictly economic motivations. But there are other, more subtle forces at work as well. These stem from the very nature of industrial production and from the scientific values that undergird industrial society.

David Landes has pointed out, in his monumental study of technical change, *The Unbound Prometheus,* that technological changes are closely intertwined with changes in the organization of production. "Factory discipline," writes Landes, "required and eventually created a new breed of worker, broken to the inexorable demands of the clock. It also held within itself the seeds for further technological advance, for control of labor implies the possibility of the rationalization of labor. From the start, the specialization of production functions was pushed further in the factory than it had been in shops and cottages; at the same time, the difficulties of manipulating men and materials within a limited area gave rise to improvements in layout and organization."[6]

In other words, production technologies not only combine energy and raw materials in the manufacture of goods, but they also provide the means by which labor forces are rationalized and controlled. David Dickson puts the case more directly: "Contemporary technology has been developed in industrialised societies in a way that seeks to secure maximum control over labour, as much as maximum production of goods."[7]

This view of technological change suggests that the development of new technology tends to build upon and reinforce the existing social and political relationships within society. Technology, in short, is part and parcel of the hierarchical power structure of industrial societies. Moreover, the development of increasingly complex and centrally-controlled technological systems, according to this interpretation, tends to increase the importance and influence of small groups of experts at the center of political and corporate power.

A similar impact is frequently seen when technologies developed in the industrial countries are transferred into the developing world. The transfer of tractors into rural areas where there are wide disparities in wealth and economic power, for example, has often resulted in increased incomes for the farmers who could afford to buy the machines, while small farmers and sharecroppers have been forced off the land as the large farms expanded. Modern industries in Third World cities have also tended to fragment and destroy local networks of small businesses, resulting in greater wealth for those associated with the modern sector and relatively poorer conditions for those outside it. Of course, technological change is not always detrimental in its social impacts. But no technology—however "appropriate"—can by itself change the social and political structures that underpin many problems.

These interpretations of technological development provide important insights into the processes of technological change, and each of them helps explain why innovation has become so central to industrial society. Yet none provides a convincing framework, on its own, to account for every facet of technological change. The reason is that technological, economic, and political forces are all involved in one way or another, and they interact to produce a complex array of pressures that push and pull technological development along certain paths.

Society is thus not simply a product of its technology. Rather, the dominant economic, political, and social forces acting in society guide the direction of technological change. David Noble, a historian at the Massachusetts Institute of Technology, sums up the process succinctly: "Technical imperatives define only what is *possible*, not what is *necessary;* what *can* be done, not what *must* be done. The latter decisions are social in nature. Unfortunately, this distinction between possibility and necessity is lost on most contemporary observers, and with it a large measure of imagination and social vision."[8]

An understanding of the forces that lead to technological change helps explain how it is that humanity has acquired such spectacular technological prowess yet continues to face problems that seem to defy technological solution. Part of the reason is that many of the problems are political, economic, or social rather than technological. Technological fixes can overcome strictly technological problems, such as how to improve the efficiency of an automobile engine, but they cannot solve wider political problems, such as how to reduce public dependence on automobiles.

Modern technology thus reflects the economic and political forces that have dominated industrial society in the past few decades. These forces have shaped the world's research and development system, guided the application of new scientific knowledge, and influenced much technological development in the Third World. But in the past few years, many of these forces have themselves changed fundamentally, as energy prices have soared, economic growth has slumped, and public resistance to the growing power of big government and large corporations has found widespread political expression. Thus, many of the technologies developed in the postwar era have become inappropriate in a fundamentally changed world.

The ancient story of Hephaestus, the lame Greek god of fire and metalworking, provides many symbols for the role of science and technology in the eighties. Hephaestus was one of the ugliest and most irascible of the gods and was often disliked. He was twice cast from Olympus, once by his mother, Hera, who cast him out at birth because she was disgusted with his appearance, and the second time by Zeus, who was angry with him for siding with his mother in a conjugal dispute. (This second fall from Olympus, according to some accounts, was responsible for his limp, for he is said to have broken his legs when he landed on the island of Lemnos.) Yet, in spite of the antipathy that many of the other gods displayed toward Hephaestus, he was eagerly sought after for his technological skills. Hephaestus was an architect, a smith, an armorer, a chariot-builder, and an artist. He fashioned delicate works of art, furnished weapons, and provided transportation in the form of the golden shoes with which the gods moved through the air. In short, he was a central and indispensable part of the workings of Olympus.[9]

2

Technology in a New Era

Sometime in the early seventies, the postwar era drew to a close. No single event marked its passing, and only in retrospect has it become clear that the world went through fundamental changes in those years. But it is now evident that shifts in the international balance of economic and political power, abrupt changes in the world oil market, rising levels of inflation and unemployment, and the emergence of new social values and aspirations all contributed to an irreversible transformation in global affairs. This transformation has had major direct and indirect impacts on the climate for technological change.

Two events in particular—the 1969 moon landing and the 1973–74 oil embargo—symbolized the deep changes that had taken place. The moon landing, the pinnacle of a long and complex effort, demonstrated humanity's technological prowess in no uncertain terms. It was a spectacular reminder of the success of the scientific and technological programs that were launched throughout the industrial world in the aftermath of World War II. But just four years later, the oil embargo demonstrated the vulnerability of the industrial countries' petroleum-based economies; it exposed the vital links between the very technologies that had been at the core of industrial expansion and a finite resource whose control had largely passed into the hands of a few oil-producing countries. The embargo signalled the end of an extraordinary era of cheap energy.

Abrupt shifts in the geopolitics, and hence the economics, of oil were not the only signs that the world was undergoing fundamental and irreversible changes. The decade that began with men walking on the moon and which ended with men and women waiting in line for gasoline also saw the postwar economic boom sputter to an end. A quarter-century of unprecedented economic growth gave way to a series of recessions, high rates of inflation, and lengthening unemployment lines. And as the decade advanced, hopes for a return to the postwar trends gradually dimmed.

Another sign that the postwar era had ended was the fact that the United States emerged from the seventies as no longer the undisputed world economic leader. During the past decade, Japan and some European countries began to offer a serious challenge to the United States in world markets—particularly those for high-technology goods in which American companies had long been dominant—and the balance of economic power shifted perceptibly away from the North American continent. A few developing countries began to penetrate markets in the industrial world with exports of manufactured goods, a development that heightened economic competition and altered the postwar structure of international economic relationships.

In many areas, these transformations, problems, and discontinuities have heightened the need for innovation. One urgent and obvious need, for example, is to move quickly away from the postwar patterns of energy production and consumption, a task that will require new energy-conserving technologies and the development of new resources. And the increased competition in markets for high-technology goods provides a major incentive for companies to innovate in order to maintain their products at the cutting edge of new technology—an incentive that is also causing many governments to pay attention to ways in which they can support their high-technology industries. Yet the economic downturn has simultaneously raised the need for new technologies and dampened the climate for innovation; for high levels of inflation and sluggish economic growth have depressed spending on research and development in some fields, and they have made many companies unwilling to commit large amounts of capital to new processes.

In any case, recent experience has shown that the technological formulas that appeared to work so well in the fifties and sixties no longer seem capable of producing the required results. Simply pouring money into the development of new technologies—in the manner of the effort to land a man on the moon—cannot solve the energy crisis, produce a cure for cancer, or overcome hunger and malnutrition. And even if there were a resurgence of innovation by industrial corporations, it is unlikely that there would be a return to the felicitous combination of high rates of economic growth, low levels of inflation, and virtually full employment that characterized much of the quarter-century following World War II.

The reasons are complex, but they are rooted in the fact that many of the most pressing problems now facing the world are as much social and political as technological. Attempts to solve energy problems by force-feeding the development of nuclear power or by burning more coal, for example, have clashed with new social values that place a premium on safety and environmental preservation. And efforts to increase food production in developing countries by the use of tractors, high-yielding varieties, and farming systems appropriate to industrial countries have raised grain yields, but they have done little to improve the nutrition of hundreds of millions of the world's poorest people—small farmers, the landless, and urban slum dwellers.

Current systems for generating and applying new technologies were established in the economic and political climate of the fifties and sixties, and they are slow to adapt to new realities. The world has changed fundamentally, but technological systems have changed little. As a 1980 report by the Organisation for Economic Cooperation and Development (OECD) has put it: "Technical advance cannot be taken for granted. Neither the rate nor the direction can now be regarded as satisfactory. The rate has slowed down substantially, and . . . the direction has meant that it is lacking in some areas where it is vitally needed."[1]

The End of Cheap Oil

Nowhere are these issues more prominently displayed than in the upheavals in world energy markets and in the responses of governments to the energy crises that have erupted in the past decade. The upheavals conveyed two clear messages: the western industrial countries, together with many developing countries, have become critically dependent on a politically volatile region of the world for a substantial fraction of their oil supplies, and the long period of stable energy supplies and prices that stretched back for almost three decades has abruptly ended. The responses to these upheavals have had an equally clear implication: there is no technological fix, whether it be a massive program to develop nuclear power or a crash effort to produce synthetic fuels, that will ensure independence from imported oil or provide immunity from higher energy prices.

The 1973–74 oil embargo and the associated rise in oil prices forcefully demonstrated the deep structural changes that had taken place in the world oil market over the previous decade. Between 1950 and 1973, world oil production increased from 4 billion to 20 billion barrels per year, climbing at a steady 7 percent annual rate. This gusher of cheap oil—its price declined substantially in real terms in this period—was poured into the growing automobile fleets, residential and industrial boilers, chemical factories, and electricity-generating plants of the industrial world. Energy-intensive technologies developed in this period helped change the shape of cities, factories, and daily lives. But these developments carried a hidden price: growing dependence on oil suppliers halfway around the world.

Until 1970, oil production in the United States, the world's most voracious consumer, expanded steadily to meet most of the nation's growing demand. These domestic supplies were supplemented by imports that came mostly from Canada and Latin America. But in 1970, production from American oil wells peaked and began to decline, while demand kept on growing. As a result, the United States turned increasingly to the Middle East to fill the widening gap between its need for oil and its capacity to produce it. Europe and Japan had long been dependent on Middle Eastern suppliers for much of their oil imports, with Japan importing almost 100 percent of its requirement. This growing dependence was made painfully apparent when Arab oil producers shut off supplies to the United States and some European countries in 1973, and the Organisation of Petroleum Exporting Countries (OPEC) abruptly quadrupled the price of its product.[2]

The events of 1973–74 sparked a good deal of consternation in the industrial countries and prompted a sheaf of studies on the world oil outlook. The realization had finally begun to sink in that industrial technology had become dangerously dependent on a source of energy that would eventually run out and that the patterns of production and consumption established during the fifties and sixties would be unsustainable over the long term. How long it would take before world oil production peaked and began to decline became a matter of intense debate, but the consensus during the late seventies was that the downturn would begin within twenty years.[3]

In the meantime, world oil demand slackened. The 7 percent growth rate of the sixties dropped to about 2 percent a year, and oil prices failed even to keep pace with inflation between 1974 and 1978. The oil crisis dropped out of the headlines. But the Iranian Revolution provided another sharp reminder of the instability of world oil supplies.

The tight oil market that had been predicted for the nineties appeared abruptly in 1979, when Iranian production was sharply curtailed. Although less than 3 million barrels of oil per day were removed from the world market—an amount equivalent to only about 5 percent of global consumption—the loss was sufficient to transform a small glut into a shortage. OPEC members, taking advantage of the shortfall, boosted prices from $13.77 to $28.45 per barrel between January 1979 and January 1980. In a decade, the price of oil had jumped by a factor of 15.[4] Cheap energy, which had exerted a major influence on technological change for a generation, had finally passed into history.

The disruptions in the world oil market that marked the close of the seventies underscored a key point: political as well as physical limits will determine the amount and cost of oil flowing in the world's tankers and pipelines during the next two or three decades. Although the physical depletion of oil reserves will inevitably cause oil production to decline in some countries—such as the United States, Venezuela, Romania, and perhaps the Soviet Union—in many others, production will deliberately be kept below maximum levels.

There are sound reasons for such a policy. For one thing, oil in the ground is a more dependable asset than are shrinking dollars in the bank. And for another, many oil producers have come to realize that their economic and political goals are best met by gearing their oil income to their development needs. That was the declared intention of the Iranian government following the downfall of the Shah, and Mexican President Lopez Portillo announced that, in developing his country's new-found oil riches, "output should be kept down to levels commensurate with the country's ability to absorb the resulting massive revenues."[5] Kuwait, Iran, Iraq, Saudi Arabia, and Bahrain have all limited their production to levels well below their maximum capacity.

In addition to planned production limits, sudden and unexpected curtailment of oil supplies is an ever present threat. The Iran-Iraq war in late 1980, for example, again removed some 3 million barrels of oil per day from the world market, and the hostilities threatened to spread to other oil producing countries. A major calamity could result from a shutdown of the Strait of Hormuz (at the mouth of the Persian Gulf) for it would choke off some 40 percent of the Western world's oil supplies. And a revolution or abrupt change of policy in Saudi Arabia could have a devastating impact on world oil markets.

Saudi Arabia is the world's largest oil exporter, accounting for about 15 percent of global production, and it is sitting atop almost one-third of the world's proven oil reserves. It is the pivotal power in the world oil market, for it can adjust its production rates to keep total supply and demand in balance and it has the greatest potential of any nation to increase its production in future years. "The massive dependence of the industrial world on one fragile regime is a frightening fact of modern life," states Harvard Business School Professor Robert Stobaugh.[6]

The seventies thus saw a dramatic and fundamental change in the world's energy picture. A quarter-century of steadily growing demand for oil and of steadily expanding production gave way to a series of upheavals, sharp price increases, and a growing precariousness in global oil supplies. The outlook for the next decade and beyond gives little cause for optimism, for even without a major disruption in supplies, markets are expected to remain tight and prices are sure to increase rapidly. Surveying the prospects late in 1980, the U.S. Office of Technology Assessment concluded that "it is highly likely that there will be little or no increase in world production of oil from conventional sources."[7]

These developments have had a variety of direct and indirect impacts on science and technology. The most obvious is the painful demonstration that scientists and engineers hold no simple technological solutions to the world's energy problems: the expectation, built up during the fifties and sixties, that the Oil Age would dissolve smoothly into the Atomic Age, has foundered on the harsh experience of the seventies. And while governments continue to pour vast sums into the development of major technologies such as the production of synthetic fuels and the construction of experimental nuclear breeder reactors, it has become clear that such programs alone cannot buy salvation from escalating oil prices. Each new technology spawns a host of new social, political, and economic problems.[8]

All of this has affected public attitudes toward science and technology, for large-scale energy projects have become the most prominent symbols of the negative side effects of technological advance, and they have become the major battlegrounds on which new social and environmental values have clashed with the technocratic, growth-oriented values that have shaped industrial society for several generations.

The fate of President Nixon's highly publicized Project Independence demonstrates the impossibility of trying to perpetuate the patterns of energy consumption established in the postwar era by relying on massive technological programs to bring forth new energy supplies. Launched in 1973, in the wake of the oil embargo, Project Independence was designed to make the United States independent of imported oil by 1985, chiefly by boosting nuclear power, coal, and domestic oil and gas production. (Nixon initially stunned even his own advisers by announcing that independence would be achieved by 1980, but the target was quickly moved ahead five years.) Announced with the same fanfare that surrounded President Kennedy's pledge of a decade earlier to put a man on the moon —and using a similar approach—Nixon's appeal to the wizardry of American technology was far less successful.

Instead of becoming less dependent on foreign oil, the United States increased its imports substantially during most of the seventies. By 1978, imported oil accounted for almost half the nation's oil consumption, compared with less than one-third when Project Independence was launched. Nuclear power, the centerpiece of the project, suffered severe setbacks as public opposition mounted, construction costs escalated, major uncertainties surrounding waste disposal and safety remained unresolved, and, with the accident at Three Mile Island, public fears deepened. The development of coal and oil shale resources also ran into a daunting array of environmental and economic barriers. The estimated cost of producing synthetic fuels from coal and shale, for example, has risen even faster than the price of oil, and the projected contribution of these fuels to domestic energy supplies has slipped steadily. The harsh lesson of the Project Independence fiasco was this: the United States may well have the technological capacity to achieve energy independence by a crash program to develop energy supplies, but exercising that capacity is not politically, environmentally, or socially acceptable.

For many scientists and engineers, the difficulties encountered by attempts to boost conventional and nuclear energy technologies are not easy to accept. Accustomed to the well-defined world of facts, figures, and risk analyses, scientists have often argued that those who oppose nuclear power, synthetic fuels plants, and similar technological projects, display an anti-scientific or anti-technological attitude. Yet solar energy and energy conservation, which enjoy popular support among those who question the desirability of pushing ahead with massive, centralized energy-development programs, themselves require the development of a range of sophisticated new technologies. Indeed, the path to increased energy efficiency and greater reliance on renewable energy resources is no less technologically challenging than one that emphasizes growth in conventional energy production and consumption.

The example of the American automobile industry indicates the scale of the technological changes needed to adjust from an era of cheap oil to one in which oil prices are climbing sharply. During the fifties and sixties, American automobiles became heavier, more powerful, and laden with energy-consuming accessories. Technological innovation in this era consisted mostly of annual changes in body design. As a result, the average energy efficiency of new cars dropped steadily; in 1973, when the oil embargo struck, Detroit was producing its most inefficient range of cars in almost half a century. But in the past few years, prodded first by government regulations and then by threats of bankruptcy, the industry has been transforming its products. Technological change has been more rapid than at any time in the automobile industry's history, and by 1985, the average car rolling off the assembly lines will get more than twice as many miles per gallon as did its predecessor of a decade earlier.[9]

Between 1975 and 1985, the industry will have spent some $80 billion on new assembly plants, and it will have made technological changes ranging from the development of minicomputers for the control of engine performance, to the manufacture of lighter body components. In industry after industry, similar efforts will be required to transform technologies developed in an era of $2-a-barrel oil to technologies suitable for an era when oil costs $50 a barrel. As a study by the U.S. National Academy of Sciences concluded, "a low-energy future offers strong incentives for technological innovation. . . . The techniques used to bring about energy reductions reported in this study in almost every case rely on the use of advanced technology."[10]

The Academy committee's central conclusion was that the

United States could enjoy strong economic growth while holding its demand for energy virtually constant or, under some conditions, even reducing its overall energy consumption. The key to these projections is the use of strong energy conservation measures and the development of new technologies that use energy more efficiently.

In many respects, such projections are based on a trend that appeared in the seventies, a trend that represents a marked break with postwar patterns of energy consumption and economic growth. Throughout the fifties and sixties, energy consumption and economic growth were tightly linked in the industrial countries. Each percentage increase in gross national product was matched by a similar percentage increase in energy demand. But by the late seventies, energy consumption was increasing at about half the rate of GNP growth in many countries: the links between energy demand and economic growth were not as strong as they appeared to be in the postwar era.

The energy crises that emerged during the seventies have thus raised a host of issues in which science and technology play a central role. But underlying the fierce debate over energy policy that has erupted throughout the industrial world is a clash of values. Choices of energy supply technologies, and decisions to stimulate energy conservation, are not simply technological matters. They involve a complex array of economic, social, political, and environmental issues. Not only have the energy upheavals of the seventies ushered in a new energy era, but they have also exposed the wider context in which technological decisions are made.

From Abundance to Scarcity

For a generation raised on the heady brew of cheap resources and rapidly advancing technology, the energy crisis of the early seventies came as quite a shock. It provoked a searching inquiry into the finite nature of global resources and the capability of technology to overcome limits to growth. But the changing energy picture was not the only indication that the world was in the midst of a transition from abundance to relative scarcity in a few vital areas.

The early seventies saw a sudden and disturbing deterioration of the world food economy, as reserve stocks dwindled to almost nothing and widespread starvation appeared in Africa and Asia. The immediate cause of the scarcity was a combination of poor harvests in the Soviet Union, the Indian subcontinent, and sub-Saharan Africa, together with a decision by the Soviet government to make up its shortfall of grain by record purchases from the United States. The world food economy improved in the late seventies, however, thanks to a string of good harvests, but as the world entered the eighties, there were gathering signs of further shortages.[11]

These ups and downs in the availability of food on the world market were primarily caused by climatic fluctuations, but they masked a dangerous underlying trend. In the quarter-century following World War II, the world grain harvest nearly doubled, climbing from 685 million tons to 1.35 billion tons. This unprecedented increase was sufficient to keep food production at least a half step ahead of demand from a rapidly swelling world population. But by the mid-seventies, one of the prime sources of increasing crop production had virtually been exhausted, for almost all the world's available cropland had been brought under cultivation. Indeed, in the past few years, there have been warning signs that some of the land now in cultivation is deteriorating, as soil erosion has reached unsustainable levels in many regions.[12]

This means that virtually all the increase in food production for the foreseeable future will have to come from raising yields per acre, a prospect made especially difficult by the fact that all the yield-increasing technologies introduced in the past few decades—fertilizers, pesticides, herbicides, and irrigation—are energy-intensive. A projection published by the U.S. government puts the task in perspective: "In the early 1970s, one hectare of arable land supported an average of 2.6 persons; by 2000 one hectare will have to support 4 persons."[13]

These global estimates hide yet another fundamentally important feature of the world food economy that has developed over the past generation: the growing dependence on North America. On the eve of World War II, only Western Europe was a major importer of grain; most other regions of the world were at least self-sufficient. But during the past quarter-century, fewer and fewer countries have been able to meet their grain needs through domestic production, and they have turned increasingly to the United States and Canada to fill the gap. By the mid-seventies, North America was the only region of the world with a substantial food surplus; its exports accounted for about two-thirds of the global grain trade. This heavy dependence on North American croplands has made grain importers everywhere dangerously vulnerable to shifts in the weather patterns (and shifts in the agricultural policies) of a single climatic region.

It is not just in terms of crop production that the world food prospect has undergone a major transformation in the past decade. As Lester Brown has pointed out, the per capita production worldwide of fish, beef, and mutton all peaked during the seventies, and have now begun to decline. These trends raise the need for new technologies to boost food production in the years ahead. But the experience of the past generation has shown that new technologies alone will not be enough to ensure that food is available to those who cannot afford to buy it. These trends have sobering implications for the food outlook in the eighties and beyond.[14]

Water is another resource whose abundance has been taken for granted in past decades but which may become increasingly scarce in the years ahead. Richard Barnet argues in his book *The Lean Years* that "because water is so obviously a finite and scarce resource, and because there are always competing drinkers, irrigators, and industrial users for the same water, conflict is inevitable." Yet water, like energy, has for decades been taken for granted. Technological development has consequently treated it as a "free good," a renewable resource whose cost could virtually be ignored in the planning of new projects. Its real value will only become obvious when, like energy, reservoirs become depleted. The report of the *Global 2000* study, a major U.S. government projection of resource and environmental trends to the end of the century, estimates that demand for fresh water worldwide will increase by between 200 and 300 percent during the final quarter of the twentieth century. "Much of the increased demand for water will be in the (developing) countries of Africa, South Asia, the Middle East, and Latin America, where in many areas fresh water for human consumption and irrigation is already in short supply," the study notes.[15]

In the industrial countries, too, competition for water supplies between industrial uses, energy production, urban expansion, and agriculture is likely to intensify. The western United States, which has extensive untapped energy resources, large areas of irrigated agriculture, and rapidly expanding cities, is likely to see increasing competition for water supplies in the years ahead. Already, water is in short supply. The waters of the Colorado River, the lifeline of the arid Southwest, are almost fully used, and there is little scope for meeting further demands. More worrying, the Ogallala aquifer, an underground reservoir that supplies irrigation water for a large area of the western plains, is showing signs of depletion. Some 40 percent of the grain-fed beef raised in the United States are fattened in an area dependent on the Ogallala, notes science writer John Walsh, but "engineering studies indicate that underground water in this region may be depleted in three to twenty years."[16]

Renewable resources, by definition, are not supposed to run out. But during the seventies, evidence mounted that so-called renewable resources in many regions were under severe pressure as rising demands began to push biological systems to the limits of their productive capacity and beyond. The deteriorating soils in many parts of the world, declining fish catches, and deforested hillsides bear witness to these trends. But the resource that is in perhaps the most parlous state in some regions is wood. Study after study has indicated that tropical forests are shrinking at an alarming rate under the pressure of rising demand for agricultural land, commercial logging operations, and the collection of firewood. This has already resulted in severe social and ecological problems in many areas, as firewood prices have soared, and as soil erosion has accelerated on deforested hillsides. As a result, the *Global 2000* study concludes that "the real prices of wood products—fuelwood, sawn lumber, wood panels, paper, wood-based chemicals, and so on—are expected to rise considerably. . . . In the industrialized nations the effects may be disruptive, but not catastrophic. In the less developed countries, however, wood is a necessity of life. Loss of woodlands will force people in many LDCs to pay steeply rising prices for fuelwood and charcoal or to spend much more effort collecting wood—or else to do without."[17]

The transition from abundance to scarcity was predicted even before the energy crisis of the early seventies, with the 1972 publication of *Limits to Growth*. A computerized study of the world economy and global resources, it essentially concluded that continued economic growth would result in serious resource depletion, coupled with rising levels of pollution. The study sparked a heated controversy; it came under heavy fire for ignoring the potential for technological change to break through the planetary limits that lie ahead. Technology, after all, had overcome shortages of food, energy, and raw materials in past centuries, and there was no reason to expect that it would not be able to repeat the performance in the future.[18]

The *Limits to Growth* may indeed have been unduly pessimistic in some respects. But impending, if not actual, shortages of both renewable and nonrenewable resources place a heavy burden on technological change. The energy-intensive, environmentally disruptive technologies developed in an era of cheap and abundant resources are contributing to some of the problems that have emerged in the past decade. Changes in technological direction have become imperative.

A New Economic Environment

Even before the upheavals in world oil markets broke the postwar patterns of energy production and use, there were signs of mounting stress in the world economy. Inflation began to accelerate in most countries in the late sixties, and unemployment levels began to climb. But the abrupt rise in oil prices in 1973–74 exacerbated these trends, ushering in a period of sluggish economic growth, global inflation, and mounting unemployment that has stretched into the early eighties and shows little sign of ending.

Technological innovation is widely viewed as a solution to many of these economic problems, for new technologies have traditionally helped boost economic growth by providing new ways to produce goods more cheaply. But innovation itself is more difficult to achieve in a depressed economic climate, and in any case, there is no reason to expect that a return to postwar patterns of innovation will be any more successful than a return to postwar economic planning in overcoming the economic · problems of the eighties.

The symptoms of global economic malaise are easy to describe, but the underlying causes are difficult to diagnose. The most obvious symptom is a global inflation rate that continues to accelerate. Inflation, which has appeared throughout history in individual countries in times of war, poor harvests, and similar periods of stress, has become a global phenomenon.[19] It affects even the centrally planned economies, where control of prices should make them less vulnerable to inflationary pressures. (See Table 2.1.)

Table 2.1. Average Annual Rate of Inflation in Selected Groups of
Countries

Country group	1960–70	1970–80
	(PERCENT)	
Low-income countries	3.0	10.7
Middle-income countries	3.1	13.1
Industrialized countries	4.2	9.4
Capital-surplus oil exporters	1.2	22.2

Source: World Bank.

At the same time, the global economy has lost much of the
buoyancy it displayed in the postwar years. The combined gross
national product of the western industrial countries and Japan
grew by more than 4 percent a year in the fifties, and by more
than 5 percent a year between 1960 and 1973. But from 1973
to 1979, the industrial economies grew by only 2.5 percent a
year, and they entered the eighties in a state of recession.
Similar trends were evident in the Soviet Union and Eastern
Europe, where annual growth rates slumped from 9.5 percent
to 6.5 percent, and finally to 5.5 percent during the same
periods of time.[20]

The oil-importing developing countries also saw their economic growth rates slow down in the seventies. Between 1965
and 1973, in spite of rapid increases in their populations, they
boosted economic output per capita at a 3.7 percent annual
rate. But between 1975 and 1978, their per capita growth rates
slumped to 2.3 percent a year. Among the hardest hit were the
poorest African countries, whose per capita growth rates
dropped from 1.6 percent a year in the sixties to just 0.2
percent in the seventies. "On average their people are as badly
off at the end of the decade as they were at the beginning,"
stated a 1980 report by the World Bank.[21]

One consequence of the slowdown in growth rates and of
efforts to dampen inflation has been a surge in global unemployment. Each year since 1975, the total number of jobless
people has increased in Europe, and in 1980, more than 20

million were out of work in Western Europe, North America, and Japan combined. In the developing world, unemployment and underemployment has reached epidemic proportions, as the number of jobs created in industry has fallen hopelessly short of the growth in the number of people looking for work. While accurate estimates are difficult to make, the International Labor Office suggested that in the late seventies, close to a half-billion people were unemployed or severely underemployed in the developing countries. "Chronic high unemployment seems to have become entrenched in most of the world economy, and traditional measures for combatting it appear inadequate or inappropriate—or both," Kathleen Newland noted in a 1979 study of world unemployment problems.[22]

These high rates of unemployment in the industrial world make labor-saving technological change—the basis of much of the rise in productivity in the postwar period—both more difficult and socially divisive. And the jobs crisis in the Third World calls into question the advisability of basing development programs on the use of labor-saving technologies imported from the industrial countries.[23]

While the economies of individual countries have encountered a combination of seemingly intractable problems, international economic relations have also undergone major upheavals. The early seventies saw the breakup of the international financial arrangements that were established at the end of World War II, under which currency exchanges were nominally fixed to the price of gold. The system began to crumble in 1971, when President Nixon took the United States off the gold standard, an action that effectively devalued the dollar against other major currencies. And the postwar arrangements collapsed completely in 1973, when exchange rates were allowed to float.

There followed a period of violent fluctuations in international financial markets, and many governments were forced to take painful steps, such as tightening credit and reducing government expenditures, in order to stabilize their currencies. The fluctuations led to changes in terms of trade; those countries whose currencies were effectively devalued saw the cost of their imports rise, thereby adding to inflationary pressures, and those countries whose currencies rose found it more difficult to boost their exports.

These gyrations in international economic affairs were already under way before the 1973–74 oil price increases, but those increases added to the instability. They prompted the largest international transfer of capital in history, and the oil-exporting countries ran up current account-surpluses of more than $60 billion in 1974. Some of this money—which rapidly became known as petrodollars—was returned to the industrial countries through purchases of capital equipment, technology, and consumer goods, and some was recycled through deposits in private western banks. The boost in oil prices that occurred in 1979 has again thrown immense strains on the international financial system. The combined surpluses of the oil-exporting countries amounted to about $110 billion in 1980.[24]

This unprecedented international movement of capital has had widespread repercussions. It has aggravated the balance-of-payments problems of many oil-importing countries, especially of developing countries, which were faced with a combined oil bill of some $47 billion in 1980. It has greatly increased international competition in export markets, as countries seek to raise their export earnings in order to pay for oil imports. And it has vastly increased the role of private commercial banks in the international economic system. Private banks have played a key role in recycling petrodollars, and they have made huge loans to developing countries to help them pay their oil import bills. By mid-1979—before the oil-price rises took place—developing countries had built up a combined debt of $221 billion to commercial banks, with Brazil alone owing more than $35 billion. The interest payments on these huge sums of money were beginning to strain the finances of many countries by the end of the seventies, raising concerns for the overall viability of the international monetary system.[25]

The economic problems and dislocations that have surfaced in the past decade are closely interlinked, and they have severed the economic trends and international financial relationships that persisted for a quarter-century after World War II. They have also deeply affected the environment for technological change. The slowdown in economic growth and constraints on government spending have reduced the growth in expenditures on research and development in many countries. In addition, according to a study by the Organisation for Economic Cooperation and Development, "the stagnant economic climate has been attracting R&D in most sectors towards the short-term and the safe." In an era of slow growth and economic uncertainty, private industry is more reluctant to make investments in new technologies to increase productivity.[26]

For developing countries, the economic uncertainties, escalating energy prices, and heavy debt burdens accumulated in the seventies have made development programs more difficult to achieve. In particular, they have raised serious doubts about the wisdom of following the industrial world down the path toward energy-intensive systems of production and consumption, and they have led some countries to take a new look at the possibilities for developing their own energy resources.

A Restructured World Economy

The United States emerged from World War II as the undisputed world leader in industrial and technological power. Throughout the fifties and sixties, American corporations dominated world trade in high technology goods, and commentators in Europe warned repeatedly of the economic dangers inherent in the "technology gap" between the United States and the rest of the industrial world. During the seventies, however, the international distribution of technological power changed fundamentally, with Japan and some European countries offering strong competition in world markets. In many respects, these developments are not too surprising. American dominance in science and technology in the postwar years was partly a result of the fact that the country emerged from World War II with its industrial and technological capacity essentially intact. Indeed, its technological might had been considerably enhanced by massive government support during the war years and by the immigration of many leading European scientists and engineers before and after the war. The United States technological dominance was, therefore, somewhat artificial, and it was bound to erode following the successful rehabilitation of the war-torn economies of Europe and Japan.

Measured in terms of changes in the relative distribution of production among the leading noncommunist industrial countries, the economic rise of Japan and West Germany is striking. In the mid-fifties, the United States accounted for almost two-thirds of the combined production of the seven largest OECD countries, but by the mid-seventies, its share had shrunk to less than half. West Germany increased its share steadily, overtaking Britain and France in the mid-sixties, while Japan boasted unprecedented rates of growth. By 1970, Japan had become the second largest economic power in the noncommunist world; its share of total production among OECD countries increased by more than a factor of four between the mid-fifties and the mid-seventies.[27] (See Table 2.2.)

Although these trends have been a long time in the making and reflect the inevitable economic recovery of Europe and Japan, they did not become conspicuous until the global economy lost momentum in the mid-seventies. As the industrial countries tried to boost their exports in order to pay for imported oil, American corporations found themselves in a highly competitive environment. Even in domestic markets for goods such as steel and automobiles, American manufacturers en-

Table 2.2. Changes in the Share of Production Among the Seven
Largest OECD Countries, 1955–1974

Country	1955	1970	1978
	(PERCENT)		
United States	64.5	53.9	45.0
United Kingdom	8.6	6.9	6.0
France	7.8	8.6	9.3
West Germany	7.3	9.9	12.5
Canada	4.3	4.3	4.6
Japan	3.8	11.0	17.8
Italy	3.7	5.2	4.6
Total*	100.0	100.0	100.0

Sources: Organisation for Economic Cooperation and Development and World Bank.
*Total may not add to 100 because of rounding.

countered stiff competition from European and Japanese companies, and imports captured a growing share of U.S. sales. For
a nation that had held a dominant position in the world economy for more than a generation, this new economic reality
became a source of deep concern.

Just how much has the United States economic and technological leadership been eroded? The evidence is conflicting, but
it is clear that there have been deep structural changes in the
world economy during the past decade or so. Relative changes
in national technological capacity lie at the center of these
economic shifts.

In terms of productivity—a key measure of economic performance—the United States still ranks above every other
country. In 1978, French and West German workers produced
about 15 percent less than their American counterparts; Japanese workers produced about one-third less; and British workers about 40 percent less. But every country, including Britain,
has improved its productivity more rapidly than the United
States during the past quarter-century. In 1950, productivity in
the United States was more than six times higher than that in
Japan, 2.5 times higher than that in France and West Ger-

many, and almost twice that in Britain.[28] (See Table 2.3.)

There are many reasons why productivity growth rates have differed so markedly over the past decade or so. Among the contributing factors are differences in levels of investment and savings, differences in structure of labor forces, and differences in rates of inflation and unemployment. A study by the U.S. National Science Foundation has also suggested that "part of the country differences in productivity gains may stem from the fact that the United States is at a much higher level of national production than other countries and thus may possibly be experiencing the diminishing rates of return effect often associated with an increasing scale of economic activity."[29] Furthermore, when Japan and West Germany rebuilt their shattered industrial plants, they were able to use the latest, most productive technologies. Whatever the causes of the changes in relative productivity levels, however, it is clear that the leading nations of the Western world—with the exception of Britain—are becoming more homogeneous in their industrial productivity, which in turn suggests that their technological levels have also evened out. How have these shifts affected international markets for high-technology goods?

By all appearances, the United States has seen its dominant position greatly eroded. In 1980, for example, more than one car in four sold in the United States was imported. A year

Table 2.3. Gross Domestic Product Per Worker in Selected Countries, Compared with the United States, 1950–78

Country	1950	1960	1970	1978
		(PERCENT OF U.S.)		
United States	100.0	100.0	100.0	100.0
Japan	15.6	23.8	48.7	63.0
France	42.4	53.7	71.0	85.6
West Germany	39.8	56.0	71.3	85.1
United Kingdom	53.6	54.0	57.6	58.4

Source: U.S. Department of Labor.

earlier, Japan had overtaken the United States as the world's largest automobile manufacturer. By the late seventies, the American steel industry was in serious difficulties, reeling under the impact of cheaper imports from more productive mills in Japan, Europe, and some Third World countries. And in many areas of consumer electronics, Japanese companies were dominating world markets to the extent that American companies had dominated them a decade earlier.

In terms of international investments by multinational corporations, there has also been a decline in U.S. dominance, reflecting the growing economic strength of other industrial countries. According to a study by the United Nations Commission on Transnational Corporations, the American share of direct foreign investment worldwide dropped from 53.8 percent in 1967 to 47.6 percent in 1976, and Britain's share sank from 16.6 to 11.2 percent. In contrast, Japan increased its share from 1.4 to 6.7 percent, and West Germany's share rose from 2.8 to 6.9 percent. Thus, while the United States remains by far the leading source of foreign investment, some other industrial countries are increasing their overseas activities at a much faster pace.[30]

This trend is evident, for example, in microelectronics—one of the hottest high-technology areas in the past few years. In the early seventies, the United States held a virtual monopoly on this technology, but by the early eighties, American companies were encountering stiff competition from foreign manufacturers. Japanese and European corporations invested in U.S. microelectronics companies, acquiring some 15 percent of American manufacturing capacity in this field. Several Japanese corporations also established European manufacturing facilities to compete head-on with the United States and Europe in the European market.[31]

Yet, in spite of these developments, the United States retained a healthy trade balance in high-technology goods during the seventies. It exported far more in the way of computers, military equipment, aircraft, and similar sophisticated products than it imported. In 1977, its trade balance in high-technology goods amounted to $27.6 billion, while it ran up a trade deficit of $24.4 billion in other goods. American high-technology exports are clearly a crucial factor in offsetting the nation's mounting oil-import bills. Indeed, international trade in general has become increasingly important to the U.S. economy in recent years. Imports and exports combined rose from 6 percent to 12 percent of the nation's GNP between 1970 and 1980, a striking indication of the growing economic interdependence among the industrial countries.[32]

As it enters the eighties, the United States is still the world's leading economic and technological power, but its dominance is not as absolute as it was in the postwar years. The industrial countries have become more interdependent, with industrial and technological capacity more evenly divided among them. For each of them, maintaining their domestic industries at the cutting edge of new technology has become a central concern, and as the world economy has become flaccid, this concern has intensified. Technological competition from abroad has become one of the chief incentives for innovation in the industrial world.

While the western industrial countries and Japan have been building up their high-technology industries, the Soviet Union and Eastern Europe have also been pumping large amounts of resources into technological development. Although direct comparisons are difficult to make, it is believed that the Soviet Union is devoting a much larger share of its gross national product to research and development than are the western industrial countries. A study by the U.S. National Science Foundation has reported, for example, that Soviet outlays on R&D in the late seventies amounted to about 3.4 percent of the nation's gross national product, compared with about 2.2 percent in the United States. The Soviet Union, moreover, has more scientists and engineers working in R&D laboratories than has any other country.[33]

These investments of money and talent have produced some impressive results. Soviet basic research in fields such as mathematics, electrochemistry, and theoretical physics is widely regarded as among the best in the world, and in some heavy industries such as mining and metallurgy, Soviet technology is on a par with that of the western countries. But by several measures, the overall level of Soviet technology lags behind that of the Western world.

In spite of its heavy support for science and technology, the Soviet Union continues to import advanced technology from the West, while exporting very little of its own outside Eastern Europe. This reliance on technology imports was underlined in late 1979, when President Carter curtailed exports of American technology to the USSR—a decision that was prompted by the Soviet invasion of Afghanistan. Between 1970 and 1977, for example, the Soviet Union imported some $3.3 billion worth of machine tools from the West, about one-fourth of which were highly advanced, automated machines. This level of imports suggests a lag in a sector that is critical for many Soviet industries.[34]

The Soviet Union has been forced to import large quantities of oil-drilling equipment. In 1978 alone, some $1 billion worth of oil-drilling equipment was bought from Western Europe and North America to aid in the USSR's massive effort to tap its oil reserves in Siberia and offshore in the Caspian Sea. And throughout the seventies, Soviet officials went shopping for a variety of other items of advanced technology in western countries, buying entire auto and truck assembly plants, electronic equipment, steel mills, chemicals, and chemical plants. These purchases were designed to modernize Soviet industry as swiftly as possible.[35]

But in a critical area, military and space technology, the Soviet Union has made enormous advances. Indeed, a massive study prepared for the U.S. National Science Foundation suggests that the concentration of scientific and technological resources on military projects in the USSR may help explain why Soviet technology in other areas is lagging. "Much like the United States," the study suggests, "the Soviet regime has spent enormous sums on defense, aerospace, and nuclear R&D while underinvesting in industrial R&D. Nor has there been any substantial spin-off from these national security and high-technology related projects in terms of civilian applications to national needs and improvements in the quality of life. The resulting pattern has been a high concentration of talent and money in defense and space and a seriously distorted deployment of S&T [science and technology] resources."[36]

The Soviet Union's success in developing its military technologies has been both a response and a stimulus to defense-related science and technology in the United States. The vast sums of money poured into defense and space laboratories produce new technologies that in turn prompt further technological countermeasures. Indeed, the threat of Soviet military developments has always been a major factor in the planning of science and technology in the United States, a fact that was particularly evident in the late fifties and early sixties following the launching of the Sputnik satellite. And the technological arms race will continue to dominate the science and technology policies and resources of the two superpowers during the eighties (see Chapter 3). This will further distort their patterns of technological development compared to those of other industrial countries, for as the United States and the Soviet Union continue to divert a large share of their scientific and technological resources into the military, countries such as Japan and West Germany will be putting most of their scientific funds and talent into the development of technologies more closely linked to industrial development. Japan and West Germany have, in fact, already overtaken the United States in terms of the share of gross national product invested in nonmilitary research and development. This measure alone marks a significant departure from the postwar dominance of the United States in all areas of research and development.

A final area of the global economy that has undergone structural change in the past decade or so is trade between the developing and industrial countries. The rapid industrialization of a few developing countries in the sixties and early seventies has resulted in a major increase in their exports of manufactured goods, as well as an increase in the volume of sophisticated products they import from the rich countries. In other words, some developing countries have become more tightly integrated into the world economy, a development that has raised important questions concerning policies for science and technology in developing and industrial countries alike.

This growing interdependence between rich and poor countries has led many influential analysts to argue that further industrialization in developing countries and continued growth in trade will ultimately benefit both the developing and the industrial worlds. In effect, the developing countries are seen as "engines of growth," whose industrial development will lead to increased demand for products from the industrial countries and hence to increased global economic growth.[37]

Although there are doubts about how swiftly such a scenario will unfold and legitimate concerns about how the benefits of such growth will be divided (see Chapter 5), the industrialization that has already taken place in a few developing countries has raised new pressures for innovation in the industrial world. As a study by the Overseas Development Council has pointed out, "some of the more advanced semi-industrialized countries are now at a stage where they are shifting from labor-intensive industries to those using more capital and higher skills. These countries are already reorienting their exports from products such as clothing and shoes toward items such as electronics, steel, automobiles, and machinery. This suggests that less developed countries will be able to produce and sell more high-technology goods and that industrial countries will face stiffer competition for markets for goods they now produce and export. On the one hand, this shows that the basic dynamism of the world economy is at work; on the other, it implies that continuous pressure will be exerted upon the industrial economies to discover new markets, products, and processes and to introduce domestic policies to maintain their international competitiveness."[38]

In other words, the industrial countries will be faced with the need to encourage growth of those industries in which they hold a comparative advantage in the world economy—high-technology, knowledge-intensive industries such as computers, microelectronics, and biotechnology—in order to offset the decline of traditional industries faced with mounting competition from the developing countries. There will also be increased pressure for industrial countries to automate their production processes in order to reduce the labor involved in manufacturing and thereby overcome some of the comparative advantage enjoyed by developing countries with lower labor costs.

These pressures are intensified in a sluggish world economy in which all countries, rich and poor alike, are competing for a share of limited markets. That is the situation that appeared in the mid-seventies, and it is likely to persist for the next several years.

New Demands and New Values

The end of the postwar era was not marked solely by changes in energy production and shifts in economic relationships. It was also characterized by the appearance of a changed social environment. The late sixties and early seventies saw the emergence of a new set of demands and values, among the most prominent of which were rising concern about environmental degradation, growing alienation of workers stuck in boring, mindless jobs, a shift in aggregate demand away from material goods toward services, and increasing calls for the regulation of food, drugs, chemicals in the workplace, and other threats to health. Even economic growth itself, the very basis of industrial advancement for generations, came under assault as the prime cause of many of the problems facing industrial society.

The emergence of these new social values resulted from trends that had gone unrecognized for years. Their economic expression in new market demands and their political expression in increased regulation of corporate activities was partly a reaction against the forces that had shaped technological development during the postwar years. These changed values fundamentally altered the environment for technological change in the seventies and beyond.

The bruising battles that erupted over nuclear power and the siting of major energy facilities were the most conspicuous manifestations of this change in values. Energy projects that had gone essentially unchallenged during the fifties and sixties and which were widely viewed as signs of progress suddenly found themselves under serious attack. People, in short, were no longer willing to accept environmental degradation and increased hazards as the inevitable price of progress.

During much of the postwar era, the values that implicitly guided technological development largely disregarded the costs involved in environmental degradation. The preservation of clean air and water and the protection of the natural environment were accorded a relatively low value in relation to the material benefits derived from increased production and consumption. As a result, the cost of goods did not reflect the full costs to society of the environmental damage associated with their production and use.

In the absence of regulations to prevent environmental abuse—and in the absence of strong public support for such regulations—there was little incentive for either producers or consumers to assume the costs involved in protecting the environment. But in the late sixties, rising public concern over environmental degradation resulted in the passage of strong environmental protection laws throughout the industrial world. These have resulted in regulations designed to ensure that producers, and ultimately consumers, pay the costs of controlling pollution rather than allowing the costs of a degraded environment to be paid by society at large.

Of course, the passage of environmental legislation has brought governments more firmly into the business of regulating market forces by reallocating costs. A similar trend has occurred in areas such as the regulation of the safety of food and drugs and the reduction of occupational hazards. Government laws and regulations in these areas have led to the adoption of measures that probably would not have been taken simply under the push and pull of market forces.

The rising concern over environmental pollution owes much to an improved understanding of the effects of pollutants on health and a heightened awareness of the depletion of resources. It also represents a shift in demand away from strictly material goods. As Professor Lester Thurow of Massachusetts Institute of Technology points out, "environmentalism is a demand for more goods and services (clean air, water, and so forth) that does not differ from other demands except that it can only be achieved collectively."[39]

In this respect, the move toward increased environmental protection matches other trends in industrial economies. As incomes have risen, demand for collective services such as health care, education, and so on have been increasing rapidly in recent years, assuming a growing proportion of the gross national product of most industrial countries.

These shifts in consumption patterns have placed new demands on science and technology. One direct result is that industrial corporations have greatly stepped up their spending on research and development related to pollution control and energy conservation. In the United States, for example, spending on pollution-control R&D rose by 50 percent and that on energy conservation doubled between 1976 and 1978. A less conspicuous result is that, as Professor Emma Rothschild has succinctly pointed out, "consumption and production are out of joint: on the one hand, consumption is increasingly 'socialized' as demand grows for environmental goods and for collective services; on the other hand, the system of production has changed more slowly, and research is still concentrated in resource-intensive industries."[40]

One result of these trends is that governments have become more deeply involved in a broad range of economic and private activities, both as regulators of industrial practices and as providers of the collective services that have become increasingly in demand. This increased government role in economic affairs is a direct result of the growing complexity of technological society and a reaction to many of the adverse trends that took place during the postwar period of rapid economic growth. But, as the seventies progressed, and as many of the economic problems of the industrial world deepened, a reaction to the growing power of government took root. Its most stunning expression came in the 1980 American Presidential election, with the election of a conservative president and Senate majority pledged to "get the government off people's backs." These countervailing trends represented deep divisions within society and reflected a lack of consensus on the role of governments in guiding economic and technological development.

The economic and social environment of the early eighties is thus greatly different from that of a decade earlier. The series of shocks that struck the world economy during the seventies were not passing phenomena which would disappear in the wake of a resumption of economic growth and a return to the energy and economic policies of the fifties and sixties. Rather, they reflect deep structural changes and express the longer-term trends that have been germinating during the postwar years. These structural changes present a severe challenge to the economic policies of industrial and developing countries alike, and by extension, they call into question the technological policies that have influenced economic development for a generation.

3

Knowledge
and Power

As the world economy has grown flaccid and as international economic competition has intensified, politicians and industrialists alike have begun to pay more lip service to the need for new technologies to revitalize sagging industries, generate new areas of economic growth, and fend off imports. And because technological changes have helped to overcome shortages of food, energy, and raw materials in the past, future technological innovation is being counted on to overcome the planetary limits that are emerging in these areas.

For example, in words reminiscent of Harold Wilson's 1963 pledge to lead Britain through the "white heat of technological revolution," President Carter announced in his first State of the Union address that he would promote "a surge of techno-logical innovation by American industry." A few years earlier, Leonid Brezhnev, in rather more colorful terms, exhorted en-terprises in the Soviet Union to "chase after scientific and technological novelties and not to shy away from [them] as the devil shies away from incense." And the reindustrialization policies that have come into vogue in some countries in the early eighties rely heavily on technological innovation to breathe new life into faltering industries.[1] Technological change, in short, has become an imperative.

One measure of the global commitment to technological change is the size and scope of investments in research and development. In just one generation, research and develop-ment has become a highly organized, lavishly funded activity. More than $150 billion is now spent on R&D worldwide, and some three million scientists and engineers are employed in scientific laboratories. These huge financial and intellectual resources have helped accelerate the pace of technological change in the past few decades.[2]

To many people, research and development is an arcane business: scientists in white coats conducting studies that seem to bear little relationship to everyday life. But R&D, which encompasses activities ranging from the pursuit of academic knowledge about the universe to the design and development of new weapons, is an essential part of the processes of techno-logical change. An understanding of the way that R&D is organized and funded, and of the priorities reflected in the world's expenditures on research and development, is vital for an understanding of the role that technological change plays in society.

Nearly four centuries ago, Francis Bacon observed that knowledge is power. That remark is becoming increasingly relevant as governments and corporations sink vast amounts of money into R&D in order to maintain an economic or military edge over their rivals. National investments now being made in the production and application of knowledge will influence economic and political relationships among the industrial countries and between the industrial and developing worlds decades hence.

A $150 Billion Global Enterprise

Research and development was catapulted into national prominence during World War II, when science was harnessed to the war effort. Scientists working with government funds produced a dazzling array of new technologies—the atomic bomb, mass production of penicillin, radar, long-range missiles, to mention just a few—and the base was laid for a long and fruitful partnership between science and government. In the postwar years, scientists and engineers rose rapidly to positions of power and prestige in government and industry; government agencies were established to channel tax revenues into R&D laboratories; and university science and engineering departments entered a period of unprecedented expansion. By the end of the seventies, the U.S. government alone was pouring $30 billion a year into R&D.[3]

These huge sums of public money have generally supported research and development that, for one reason or another, has not been adequately funded by private industry. Academic research, military science and technology, and the space program, for example, all make substantial claims on government budgets. Just as the war effort brought science and government together in the forties, the arms race and the space race cemented their marriage in the fifties and sixties. More recently, increasing amounts of public funds have been channeled into such areas as energy production, health care, transportation, and industrial innovation, as governments have sought to enlist the scientific community in an attack on social and economic problems.

The funding of research and development by private corporations has a longer history. Vast industrial empires were built decades ago on the engineering breakthroughs of inventors such as Thomas Edison and Alexander Graham Bell and earlier entrepreneurs like James Watt and Richard Arkwright. Indeed, corporate laboratories established in the late nineteenth and early twentieth centuries became the world's earliest large-scale R&D centers. By the twenties, they employed thousands of scientists and engineers.[4]

This early industrial involvement with science and technology has blossomed into a close, even symbiotic relationship in recent decades, with the rise of new industries based on the exploitation of scientific knowledge. Basic understanding of the behavior of molecules and atoms lies at the core of such industries as electronics, communications, petrochemicals, computers, and pharmaceuticals. These science-based industries, which have been at the leading edge of industrial growth in the postwar era, all plow a significant fraction of their profits back into their laboratories in an effort to gain an edge over their competitors.

The steep rise in public and private expenditures on R&D during the past generation has been accompanied by the establishment of complex arrangements between governments, universities, and industry for the performance of R&D—arrangements that have blurred the boundaries between public and private institutions and have played a key role in shaping the priorities in the global research and development budget.

In most of the western industrial countries, between 40 and 50 percent of total national expenditures for R&D come directly or indirectly from government agencies, and in developing countries the share is even higher. Only a relatively small fraction of this money is generally spent in government laboratories, however. The rest is channeled into universities and private corporations.

Government support for research and development in the universities is mostly devoted to basic research—research that is designed to push back the frontiers of knowledge, but for which there is no immediate practical application in sight. In the past few decades, most countries have established arrangements whereby university researchers receive government funding in the form of grants and contracts, and thus governments have gradually assumed the leading role in supporting academic science. These government-university research links have been enormously valuable in advancing scientific research and in supporting higher education in general, but they have also raised some problems.

In the United States, for example, the huge expansion of university research in the past few decades has fundamentally altered the character of higher education. As science writer Daniel Greenberg has observed, "Congress . . . permitted 'research' to become the vehicle for pouring federal assistance into the university system. And, not surprisingly, research, with its own mores, values, and rewards, tended to overwhelm the educational function of many universities." This heavy dependence on government support has also made research vulnerable to oscillations in government expenditures and to abrupt shifts in priorities.[5]

In addition to funding R&D to advance their own commercial objectives, private corporations in the western countries also carry out a wide range of research and development activities under contract to government agencies. Willis Shapley, a veteran observer of R&D policy in the United States, described these activities concisely:

[Companies] are developing weapons systems, space hardware, energy technologies, and new medicines; they are doing applied research and development on new technologies, new equipment, and new instruments; and they are building experimental and demonstration plants and federal R&D facilities. They are doing an enormous volume of paper studies of new concepts and design options, sometimes backing them up with experimental tests of crucial features.

They are providing government with a wide range of support services for federal research, development, test, and evaluation activities, ranging from full responsibility for the operation of laboratories and test centers to the provision of more specialized analysis, computational and other technical services.[6]

These government contracts for industrial R&D are heavily concentrated in a few industries—chiefly those of interest to defense, space, and energy agencies. For some corporations, federal contracts dwarf all other business, and a large amount of corporate energy is devoted to securing a steady flow of future contracts. Activities such as writing proposals, bidding on contracts, and lobbying for congressional support for specific programs take the place of promotion and advertising in the selling of the major product of these companies—scientific expertise.

Aside from these direct funding links between governments, universities, and corporations, there are also indirect linkages. Academic scientists frequently advise legislative committees and government agencies on their technological programs, and they often sit on the boards of corporations. Corporation officials also sometimes serve as government advisers, and some firms directly fund university researchers.

Research and development in the Soviet Union and Eastern Europe tends to be more highly compartmentalized than that in the West. In general, institutions connected with the Soviet Academy of Sciences concentrate mostly on basic research. These institutes tend to be large organizations concerned with research in a single scientific discipline. Applied research is largely the province of the industrial ministries, while the production enterprises—the rough equivalent of corporations in the Western world—carry out the development of new products and processes.

Although there are complex links between these three components of the Soviet research and development system, this division of responsibilities has been criticized for inhibiting the processes of technological innovation. A report by researchers from George Washington University suggests that "demand is created by top-down edicts; the force of these mandates is diluted as they are transmitted through the many, often conflicting, layers of bureaucracy."[7]

In a single generation, research and development has thus developed into a multi-billion-dollar global enterprise that binds public and private institutions together with a system of grants, contracts, and planning directives. The whole system is built around the interests of governments, corporations, universities, and research agencies which together constitute the R&D enterprise. These interests are sometimes complementary, but they are often in conflict.

The Changing Geography of R&D

These huge investments in the generation of new technology are concentrated in a handful of rich, industrial countries. In rough terms, the United States is responsible for about one-third of the worldwide expenditure on R&D. Western Europe and Japan together account for a similar fraction. And the Soviet Union and Eastern Europe combined spend just under one-third of the total. This means that the developing countries of Africa, Asia, and Latin America account for only a miniscule fraction of the world's research and development activities—less than 3 percent, according to recent estimates.[8]

It is difficult to develop an accurate picture of who spends what on research and development. Not only are national statistics often sketchy and out of date, but international comparisons are also clouded by rapidly fluctuating exchange rates, inconsistent definitions of what constitutes R&D, and differences in the makeup of national research and development programs. Nevertheless, it is clear that there has been a significant shift in the distribution of R&D expenditures among the industrial countries in the past decade or so, a shift that seems to support American fears that its technological leadership is being eroded.

In the mid-sixties, the United States accounted for about two-thirds of the total spending on R&D among the OECD countries, but by the late seventies, its share had fallen to one-half. Japan and most European countries had been expanding their outlays on R&D during a period when expenditures in the United States were severely constrained.

Additional evidence for this trend can be seen in changes in the level of gross national product devoted to R&D among the western industrial countries and Japan. In the early sixties, there was wide variation from country to country. The United States devoted a far greater share of its national income to R&D than any other country. It spent about 3 percent of its GNP on research and development, compared with 2.6 percent in Great Britain, about 2.0 percent in France, and close to 1.5 percent in West Germany and Japan. The ratio declined in the United States during the sixties and early seventies; it peaked in Britain during the late sixties and declined during the seventies; and it rose in West Germany and Japan throughout this period. By the late seventies, all the major industrial countries in the Western world were devoting between 1.8 and 2.3 percent of their gross national products to research and development.[9] (See figure, page 69.)

The change in the distribution of R&D capacity among the industrial countries was partly due to a decline in real expenditures on military R&D in the U.S. as the Vietnam war drew to a close, coupled with a sharp drop in support for space technology in the late sixties and early seventies following the successful completion of the fabulously expensive Apollo Program.[10] The steep rise and fall of the space program goes a long way toward explaining the apparent decline of the American R&D enterprise in the seventies.

As for the size of the research and development effort in the

Percent

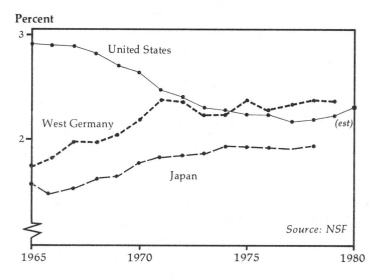

Share of GNP Spent on Research and Development

Soviet Union and Eastern Europe, there are few reliable esti-mates. The Soviet goverment's own reported spending is not directly comparable with that in western countries because there is considerable doubt about how much military science is included and it is thought to exclude some expenditures—such as prototype development—that are included in western figures. Nevertheless, estimates by both Jan Annerstedt, of Roskilde University in Denmark, and the United Nations Edu-cational, Scientific and Cultural Organisation indicate that the combined R&D spending by the Eastern bloc countries lagged only slightly behind that of the United States in the mid-seventies.[11]

Another indication of the size of the Soviet Union's research and development effort is the steady increase in the number of researchers in its labor force. According to a careful estimate by Louvan Nolting and Murray Feshbach of the U.S. Bureau of the Census, the USSR had built up the world's largest body of research scientists and engineers by the late seventies. Its scientific labor force outnumbered that of the United States by about three to two.[12] Yet, in spite of these huge investments of money and talent, the Soviet Union continues to import key technologies from the West, and aside from armaments, it exports little in the way of advanced technology.

While there have been marked shifts in the distribution of R&D spending among the industrial countries, one feature of the global research and development enterprise has remained constant: the developing countries continue to account for a tiny share of the world's scientific resources. This striking disparity between rich and poor countries is especially marked when outlays on research and development are expressed in per capita terms. In 1979, the United States spent about $200 on R&D for every person in the country, and several European countries invested close to that level. In contrast, most Latin American nations spent less than $5 per person, and the poorer countries of Africa and Asia could afford less than $1 per person.[13]

The developing countries' share of the world's pool of researchers has been growing in recent years, thanks to an expansion of university education in some countries. But the Third World has only a tiny fraction of its labor force engaged in research and development compared with the portion in the industrial world. Jan Annerstedt calculates that there were about 300 scientists and engineers working on R&D for every million workers in developing countries during the early seventies, while the industrial world had almost 4,000 researchers per million workers.

While these disparities simply mirror many others between rich and poor countries, they nevertheless have important implications. As long as the world's R&D capacity remains highly concentrated in the industrial nations, the focus will continue to be largely on the problems of the rich countries. Even in areas such as health and agriculture, global R&D programs are largely aimed at solving the problems encountered in the rich, temperate zones.

This skewed distribution of the world's R&D resources ensures that most technological development takes place in the industrial world. The developing countries have thus become deeply dependent on imported—and often inappropriate—technology for their economic development. Such dependency is aggravated when a developing country lacks sufficient expertise to evaluate and assimilate technologies offered by multinational corporations.

The World's Scientific Priorities

While it is difficult enough to estimate how much each country spends on R&D, it is even more of a problem to determine what all this money actually buys. The reason is simple: much of the world's scientific research is cloaked in secrecy—either for military or commercial reasons—and therefore is out of public view. Nevertheless, the chief priorities in the global research and development budget are clear. (See Table 3.1.)

Military R&D alone accounts for more financial and intellectual resources than are devoted to R&D on health, food production, energy, and environmental protection combined. Moreover, as the global distribution of R&D capacity implies, the world's research and development enterprise is overwhelmingly geared to meeting the political and economic goals of the industrial nations.

These priorities, which differ from country to country, are the result of a constellation of forces. The global research and development budget is the product of vested interests, whether they be corporations seeking higher profits, governments seeking greater military and political strength, or university scientists seeking larger research budgets. The R&D proposals con-

Table 3.1. The Global Research and Development Budget, 1980

Program	Share
	(PERCENT)
Military	24
Basic research	15
Space	8
Energy	8
Health	7
Information processing	5
Transportation	5
Pollution control	5
Agriculture	3
Others	20
Total	100

Source: Author's estimates based on data from national sources and international agencies. Figures are approximate and should be regarded as no more than a rough guide to relative expenditures.

tained in the yearly budgets of the U.S. government, for example, are among the most intensely analyzed and bitterly contested items, even though R&D constitutes less than 6 percent of total government outlays. The forces that shape the world's scientific priorities can be discerned from a closer examination of some of the components of the global research and development budget.

Feeding the Military Machine

The largest single item by far in the global research and development budget is the advancement of military technology. More than $35 billion, roughly one-fourth of the world's investment in R&D, was swallowed up by military programs in 1979, and over half a million scientists and engineers were working on the development of new weapons and defense systems. The feeding of the world's military machine is thus the predominant occupation of the global research and development enterprise.[14]

These colossal expenditures are largely concentrated in the United States and the Soviet Union, although military programs dominate the R&D budgets of Britain and France as well. These four nations invested heavily in military R&D in the postwar years, as the superpowers entered into an arms race and as Britain and France developed their own independent nuclear capabilities. Major weapons laboratories were established in the forties and fifties, links were forged between government agencies and private corporations as industry began to build new weapons and conduct military research under government contracts, and prominent scientists were pressed into service to advise defense agencies on their weapons programs.

Tax revenues, channeled through government agencies, provide virtually all the funds for military R&D. In the United States and Britain, more public money is spent on the development of military technology than on all other government-supported R&D programs combined; both countries devote about half their government R&D budgets to their military forces. In France, the share is 30 percent, while in Germany it is a more modest 11 percent, and in Japan it is a minuscule 2 percent.[15] (See Table 3.2.)

The military R&D effort is important not only for its huge claim on financial and intellectual resources, but also for its key

Table 3.2. Share of Government R&D Budgets Devoted to Military Programs

Country	1961	1970	1974	1976
		(PERCENT)		
United States	71	52	52	50
United Kingdom	65	41	47	48
France	44	32	34	30
West Germany	22	18	12	11
Japan	4	2	2	2

Source: National Science Foundation and European Economic Commission.

role in maintaining the momentum of the arms race. Today's R&D projects become tomorrow's expensive new weapons, in an escalation of armaments that depends as much on technological sophistication as it does on sheer numbers. Technological breakthroughs are rapidly incorporated into new weapons and defense systems, and the tempo of innovation is driven at a fast pace by the fear of falling behind in the scientific race. Thus, in an endless succession of action and reaction, technological changes in the armaments of one superpower are countered by changes in the weaponry of the other.

This heavy reliance on science and technology to boost military strength is evident in the defense budgets of the United States during the past few years. A buildup of military R&D began in the late seventies with steady real increases in budget allocations. But in the 1981 budget—released early in 1980, in the wake of the Soviet invasion of Afghanistan—these programs were singled out for a massive increase, amounting to more than 20 percent of the total spent on military R&D in 1980. The Department of Defense is scheduled to spend $16.6 billion on R&D in 1981, the Department of Energy will put another $1.3 billion into nuclear weapons research, and the National Aeronautics and Space Administration will lend more support with the development of launch vehicles and space systems that will be used both for military and civilian purposes. These outlays, moreover, will almost certainly be increased in the early eighties as the Reagan Administration carries out its pledge to expand America's arsenals.[16]

One program alone, the MX missile system, is allocated $1.5 billion in research and development money in 1981. This program is a prime example of the technological forces that govern the upward spiral in the arms race. The MX system is designed to counter what American military planners view as major advances in the accuracy of Soviet intercontinental missiles, advances that are believed to make U.S. land-based missiles vulnerable to a preemptive Soviet strike. It would consist of hundreds of miles of railways, linking empty missile silos. The idea is that missiles will be shuttled from silo to silo in an endless shell game designed to outwit Soviet spy satellites, for it will be impossible to tell which silos are occupied and which are empty, and there will be too many silos for Soviet missiles to be sure of destroying them all in a single strike. By the time it is built, this fantastic network could cost as much as $60 billion. And the MX program is only one of several efforts designed to counter the ability of the Soviet Union to launch a crippling first strike by ensuring that a large number of American missiles would survive—the trident submarine and the cruise missile are two others that will eventually cost tens of billions of dollars. Moreover, since the MX missiles themselves will be highly accurate, Soviet military planners will undoubtedly press for programs to protect their own land-based missiles from an American first strike.[17]

Technological forces are not the only ones to govern the arms race. The huge defense establishments and military-industrial links in the western countries provide a built-in constituency in favor of raising military R&D budgets. And, with the global trade in armaments now running at more than $120 billion a year, there are obvious commercial incentives for nations to keep their military hardware at the forefront of technological advancement to ensure its attractiveness on world markets. Small wonder, therefore, that the recent huge boost in the U.S. defense budget was greeted with enthusiasm on Wall Street.

Yet, the economic benefits from this military spending spree may be illusory. The manufacture of weaponry is an extremely capital-intensive enterprise that creates relatively few jobs per dollar of investment and which drains capital away from more productive uses. Moreover, those countries that invest heavily in military R&D are seeing a disproportionate share of their scientific resources devoted to programs that do not contribute much to economic or social advancement. The *Economist* recently asked, "Is it sensible for a small country like Britain to devote £800 million a year to inventing tomorrow's defense technology when its armed forces are still usually equipped with yesterday's arms and never seem to have enough money to buy today's?" The *Economist* might also have questioned the wisdom of spending so much on military R&D in view of Britain's other pressing social and economic problems.[18]

Certainly, there is often some economic and technological spin-off from the development of military technology. Many advances in civil aviation and space technology, for example, owe much to the development of military systems, and some of the early developments in microelectronics were spurred by major financial investments by the U.S. Department of Defense. But some of these developments would eventually have taken place anyway, and the heavy concentration on military technologies in some countries has diverted both funding and talent away from nonmilitary programs. Simon Ramo, founder of TRW, a major defense contractor in the United States, has argued that "in the past 30 years, had the total dollars we spent on military R&D been expended instead in those areas of science and technology promising the most economic progress, we probably would be today where we are going to find ourselves arriving technologically in the year 2000 . . . the employment of a large fraction of the best scientists and engineers on military projects means they are not available to advance the store of knowledge and innovate along nonmilitary lines. Our disproportionate share of the military weapons requirements of the noncommunist world has accordingly handicapped us by comparison with our industrialized allies."[19]

It is perhaps no coincidence that two countries with relatively small military investments, West Germany and Japan, have also had the most buoyant economies during the past decade. Indeed, these two countries now rank above the United States, Britain, and France in terms of the share of gross national product devoted to nonmilitary R&D, a position they achieved in the mid-seventies and which has almost certainly been consolidated in the past few years.[20] (See Table 3.3.) There are, of course, historical reasons why Japan and West Germany spend relatively little on military programs, for they rely heavily on the United States and NATO for their defense needs. But in terms of the impact of nonmilitary R&D on economic growth and social development, this ranking may be far more revealing than a straightforward comparison of overall expenditures on R&D.

Space technology, like military technology, has also been boosted by competition between the two superpowers. The launching in 1957 of the Soviet Sputnik satellite sent shock waves through the U.S. government, for it suggested that the Soviet Union had pulled ahead in a key area of science and technology that had obvious military implications. Research and development in the United States was consequently given a huge financial shot in the arm in an attempt to close the gap. The Apollo Program, launched by President Kennedy in 1961, was the culmination of this effort.

Although it is difficult to separate the military parts of space R&D from those designed purely for civilian and scientific purposes, it is estimated that about 8 percent of the world's research and development budget is devoted to nonmilitary

Table 3.3. Share of Gross National Product Spent on Nonmilitary R&D in Major OECD Countries

Country	1967	1975
	(PERCENT)	
France	1.65	1.45
Japan	1.28	1.69
United Kingdom	1.69	1.48
United States	1.80	1.66
West Germany	1.49	1.96

Source: Organisation for Economic Cooperation and Development.

space technology. The proportion is less than it was during the late sixties, at the climax of the Apollo Program, but it nevertheless accounts for more than $10 billion a year. The civilian space program in the United States, for example, is still the third largest item in the government's R&D budget, accounting for about $5 billion a year, and it dwarfs the total R&D programs of such countries as the Netherlands, Sweden, and Switzerland.[21]

The Soviet Union is believed to be putting more resources into its space program than is the United States. Between 1975 and 1979, there were more than 400 launches of Soviet space vehicles, compared with just over 100 American launches, for example.[22] The Soviet space effort is believed to be largely geared toward military purposes, and with the advent in the early eighties of the American space shuttle—a reusable space launcher that will be used for both military and civilian programs—the stage is set for an escalation of military space technology during the eighties and nineties.

While no other country is channeling a substantial share of its public R&D resources into space technology at present, several European countries are cooperating on the development of launchers and satellites, and there is growing commercial interest in telecommunications satellites. Japan, India, and China also have their own independent space programs. Global investments in space R&D are thus likely to continue to command a substantial portion of the world's R&D resources for the foreseeable future.

The Knowledge Business

A vast research enterprise has been established over the past few decades to develop a better understanding of everything from atoms to galaxies and from cells to humans. Basic scientific research, which by definition is undertaken with no specific application in mind, has become big business. It accounts for about $20 billion per year worldwide—roughly one dollar in every seven spent on R&D—and the conduct of research has become a major function of the world's universities.

These huge outlays on basic research have led to breathtaking advances in scientific knowledge during the past generation. In virtually every branch of science, old concepts have been discarded and new ones formulated in light of revolutionary findings and fresh theories. Backed by expensive new instruments and lavish research budgets, scientists have begun to unravel some of the mysteries of the universe, probing deeper and deeper into the heart of atoms and cells and developing a better understanding of the workings of the physical and biological universe.

In the past three decades, our view of the earth has been transformed by the knowledge that the continents are giant plates moving like rafts on the planet's surface, driven by immense forces within the crust. "Not since Copernicus displaced the Earth from the center of the universe has there been such a revolution in scientists' concept of the planet," stated the National Academy of Sciences in a 1980 report. Equally startling developments have taken place in biology. Beginning with the 1953 discovery of the nature of DNA, the genetic material that governs the processes of heredity, advances in genetics and biochemistry have provided fresh insights into the molecular workings of living things. And in the submicroscopic recesses of the atom, scientists have discovered an endless array of particles that constitute the basic building blocks of matter, and gained a deeper understanding of the forces that power the atomic furnaces of the stars.[23]

Basic research lies at one end of the broad spectrum of activities that fall under the rubric of research and development. Sometimes described as a search for knowledge for its own sake, it should be distinguished both from applied research, which is designed to unearth information with a definite use in sight, and from experimental development, which is the generation and testing of products and processes that incorporate new scientific knowledge.

The boundaries separating these three activities are in fact blurred. It is often difficult to tell where basic research ends and applied research begins and where applied research becomes experimental development. But the evolution of technology often involves a progression along the research and development spectrum. The development of atomic weapons, for example, began with the arcane studies of scientists such as Albert Einstein, Niels Bohr, and Ernest Rutherford, who probed the structure of the atom in the decades before World War II. Their seemingly esoteric research laid the base for the intensive applied research effort during the war years that culminated in the production and use of the atomic bomb.

Long considered the province of a few lone, even eccentric scientists, basic research has been transformed in the past generation into a highly organized, lavishly funded enterprise, involving large teams of researchers at work with sophisticated and expensive equipment. This transformation has been swift and dramatic. Even during the twenties and thirties, most basic research consisted of relatively small-scale studies; and, while some European work was supported by government funds, the United States invested little public financing in basic research before World War II. The wartime alliance between scientists and the military began the transformation of the basic research enterprise.

The metamorphosis was completed with heavy government investment in the postwar years, as public authorities in most countries assumed the primary responsibility for supporting basic researchers and as new channels were established for funneling tax revenues into research laboratories. In the United States, for example, the basis for federal support of academic science was laid with the publication of a 1945 report, *Science: The Endless Frontier*, written by Vannevar Bush, a senior scientist and an advisor to Presidents Roosevelt and Truman. Bush's central argument was that the government should assume responsibility for maintaining the health and vigor of American research, which had made so decisive a contribution to the war effort. In 1950, following Bush's recommendation, Congress established the National Science Foundation to channel funds to university researchers.[24]

During the following two decades, outlays on basic research rose by leaps and bounds, and they were given an additional boost by the post-Sputnik panic that swept through the American scientific enterprise in the late fifties and early sixties. During the first two decades of the postwar era, budgets increased by close to 20 percent a year above annual inflation, and the bulk of the money went into university laboratories. By the early seventies, some two-thirds of the basic research conducted in the United States was being performed in academic establishments. The federal government had become the leading source of funds for basic research, accounting for about 70 percent of the total expenditure nationwide.[25]

Most other western countries established broadly similar funding patterns during the postwar period, although in addition to pouring money into university science departments, many also set up extensive government laboratories to conduct basic research. The Soviet Union and Eastern Europe, meanwhile, established very different arrangements. About 80 percent of Soviet basic research is carried out in specialized laboratories of the Academy of Sciences, a location that separates research from teaching. A network of Academy laboratories stretches across the country, and its scientists are the best and most highly qualified scientists in the Soviet Union.[26]

The steep rise in funds for basic science during the fifties and early sixties radically transformed relationships between governments and academia. One reason for pouring research money into the universities was to encourage and support the education of scientists and engineers. From the start, healthy and vigorous science departments were seen as an essential ingredient in the training of the next generation of researchers.

Research funding became firmly tied to the annual appropriations process in many countries, which meant that long-term projects were increasingly vulnerable to short-term shifts in funding levels and to changes in overall research priorities. The time of senior researchers became increasingly taken up with writing and reviewing grant proposals to secure funding for future years, while doctoral candidates and postdoctoral students did most of the actual research work. The age of the scientist-administrator, managing a team of researchers while stumping up grant money, was launched.

While these new funding and working arrangements were being established, the research environment itself was undergoing fundamental changes. The most conspicuous aspect of the postwar change in the character of science has been the growth of what science historian Derek de Solla Price has termed "big science."[27] Nature yields its secrets grudgingly. Each new piece of scientific knowledge seems to open up a new and intriguing set of questions that require more research and more powerful scientific instruments to answer. As a result, whole branches of science now rely on complex and expensive hardware, and many teams of scientists are working on different aspects of what once seemed a single problem. The biologist with a $100 optical microscope in the thirties has become, in the eighties, a molecular biologist with a $100,000 electron microscope.

Indeed, developments in the technology of scientific instruments and giant machines often determine the pace of scientific discovery. This progression is especially evident as scientists have probed deeper and deeper into the heart of the atom. The research that began a half-century ago to determine the structure of the basic building blocks of matter is now carried out with atom smashers that cost hundreds of millions of dollars to construct and operate. In the seventies, for example, American taxpayers paid some $250 million for the construction of a large particle accelerator near Chicago, and European taxpayers funded the establishment of a machine near Geneva that cost a similar amount. Now, more powerful accelerators are required to answer new questions about the structure of atoms and the nature of the forces that bind subatomic particles together.

Similar trends have occurred in astronomy, as ever more powerful telescopes are needed to study the outer reaches of the universe and as new space vehicles are required to provide close-up views of the planets. In November 1980, for example, a $78 million telescope was put into service in the New Mexico desert and a $300 million spacecraft was on its way to Saturn to study that mysterious planet's surface.

The growth in big science and the growing dependence on government funds caused few real problems in the first two decades of the postwar years. That turned out to be a golden period in basic science. Budgets rose steeply enough to accommodate much of the rising cost of equipment and to support the booming expansion of the scientific community.

Between the mid-fifties and the mid-sixties, the number of scientists and engineers employed in American universities alone more than doubled, from 25,000 to 53,000, and by 1969 their ranks had swollen to 68,000. And graduate science departments, cranked up by the flood of federal money that had been pouring into research laboratories, were turning out record numbers of Ph.D. scientists and engineers in the late sixties. Similar, though slightly less dramatic, increases took place throughout the industrial world in the quarter-century following World War II.[28]

This burgeoning growth in budgets and in numbers of researchers was reflected in the volume of scientific literature published in research journals. By the early seventies, more than 2,000 journals were carrying research reports from the world's scientists, conveying information on the results of experiments, new theories, and new interpretations of scientific phenomena. This flood of literature—more than 300,000 research reports are published in scientific journals each year—is the chief means of communicating research results, and it is the primary means by which scientists establish priority for their findings.[29] The scientific publishing industry itself has become big business in the past few decades, and scientific papers constitute the most tangible output of the knowledge industry.

By the early seventies, however, stresses and strains began to appear in the basic research enterprise in several countries. Budgets began to level off, and scientists found themselves competing with other claimants for a share of constrained government budgets. Moreover, just as funding became tight, the arrangements by which money is channeled into research laboratories came under fire.

Scientists have consequently been quick to declare a state of crisis. In November 1978, for example, Jerome Weisner, president of the Massachusetts Institute of Technology, announced that the academic research enterprise in the United States had "begun to deteriorate and come apart so badly that we have reached a point of crisis that could see the effectiveness of the nation's major research universities seriously curtailed at a time when it sorely needs to be enhanced."[30]

Although such statements include more than a little hyperbole, there is no doubt that the basic research system has been going through a period of difficulty. At the root of the problems is money. The steep growth in financial support for basic research that had taken place throughout the postwar era tailed off in most countries in the seventies. This trend began earlier and was especially pronounced in the United States, where research support began to slow down in the late sixties. After inflation is taken into account, spending on basic research by the federal government dropped by 16 percent between 1968 and 1975. In West Germany, a 1976 report by the German Research Society stated that support for science, after years of growth, had come to a standstill; and in Britain there has been virtually no real growth in funds for basic research since the early seventies.[31]

The difficulties caused by this slowdown have been compounded by structural changes in the universities as members of the postwar "baby boom" have passed through the higher education system. Moreover, enrollments in many university science courses have declined in recent years, and universities have consequently been hiring fewer new faculty members. As a result, young scientists with newly-minted Ph.D. degrees are having a tough time finding academic research and teaching jobs. Consequently, the average age of faculty members is increasing, for those who received tenure during the boom years of the sixties are still teaching and little fresh blood is entering the system. David Davies, former editor of the British science journal Nature, has pointed out that very few academic research or teaching posts opened up in British universities in the late seventies, and as a result, a Ph.D. degree is no longer a passport to an academic job. This, in turn, Davies suggests, will probably discourage many young people from enrolling in graduate science courses, and university science departments will contract even further.[32]

In spite of these difficulties, however, there is little tangible evidence that the quality of basic research has declined. Fundamental breakthroughs continue to be made, and scientific journals continue to bulge with reports of new findings. It may be that the quality of the output from basic research simply cannot be measured and that a decline could take place without any overt indications. But by at least one indirect measure—the award of Nobel Prizes—it seems that basic research in the United States has not deteriorated in relation to that in other countries, in spite of the decline in U.S. funding. American scientists won most of the Nobel Prizes for science throughout the seventies.

One reason why the quality of basic research may not have

suffered is that the best researchers and the top-quality research centers have fared relatively well in securing funds. It is the second-rank institutions that have suffered most. That, indeed, was the conclusion of a major study, conducted in the late seventies, of academic science in the United States. It suggested that the universities would continue to face problems related to declining enrollments in science courses and warned that some of the lower-ranking institutions may be forced to drop research in some disciplines entirely, a move that would divorce research from teaching in those universities.[33]

Why do governments pour tax revenues into basic research? There is no simple explanation. Part of the reason is that a healthy research enterprise is good for national prestige and that basic scientific knowledge greatly enriches human culture. But, as John Holmfeld, a science adviser to the U.S. Congress has pointed out, "Although no one can define what the 'right' level of support for science as a cultural activity should be, it is surely exceeded by the present level." Government funding of other cultural pursuits amounts to only a tiny fraction of that devoted to basic research. Instead, suggests Holmfeld, the huge outlays on science "can only be justified in terms of an eventual technological benefit to society."[34] This expectation that the results of basic research will eventually be put to practical use has provided the most powerful impetus behind the growth of the knowledge business during the past few decades.

Energy: The New Growth Area

Although defense and space R&D still account for a huge chunk of the world's research and development expenditures, their share declined during the seventies. This is largely because spending on health and energy R&D rose sharply, especially in the United States. Between 1972 and 1979, government spending on energy R&D in the United States rose from $500 million to more than $3.5 billion—an increase of more than 300 percent even after inflation is taken into account. Outlays on health R&D rose by about 40 percent in real terms during that period, with a large fraction of the increased funding going into the much-publicized war on cancer. Yet, at the end of the decade, worldwide government spending for military R&D was still more than twice that for health and energy R&D combined.[35]

Like the Sputnik launch of 1957, the 1973–74 Arab oil embargo galvanized a few western governments into pumping large amounts of money into research laboratories. It also caused many corporations to step up their own energy R&D expenditures as well. In the four years following the embargo, outlays on energy R&D among the countries that belong to the International Energy Agency (all the major western countries except France) almost doubled in real terms. The United States reported the biggest increase—181 percent—while the other governments raised their combined spending by about one-third.[36]

In many respects, the energy research and development budgets of the Western world represent an extension of government policies during the fifties and sixties, when nuclear power was widely expected to offer a safe, cheap source of energy. Most governments sank virtually all of their energy R&D funds into nuclear energy in those years, and many expected private industry eventually to take over nuclear development. Those investments shaped the industrial world's energy policies during the seventies. Government spending on nuclear energy in most countries is now geared toward answering key questions about the safety of nuclear plants and finding ways to dispose safely of radioactive waste materials. Far from being able to turn nuclear development over to private industry, governments around the world are finding themselves faced with escalating nuclear energy research bills.

About one-third of the Western world's investment in nuclear R&D is spent on developing the breeder reactor, a nuclear plant that will generate plutonium. Breeder reactors are not expected to make much of a contribution to energy supplies before the turn of the century, just about the time when solar energy could make up a substantial share of the world's energy budget. Yet spending on breeder reactor development in 1979 was three times higher than on solar development among all International Energy Agency (IEA) members. Even in the United States, which spends more on solar R&D than the rest of the world combined, funding for breeder-reactor development is still on a par with that for solar R&D.[37] This distribution of expenditures will be even more skewed in the next few years, for the Reagan Administration has proposed sweeping cuts in spending on solar and conservation while arguing for increases in support for nuclear R&D. The Reagan Administration's energy policy is based on the notion that market forces should determine the pattern of investment in energy technologies, but this philosophy does not seem to apply to nuclear power.

The apparent preference for nuclear R&D should, nevertheless, be seen in light of the marked shifts in energy R&D priorities in many countries in recent years. For example, in the IEA member countries, the share of total government energy R&D expenditures devoted to conservation rose from 2.3 percent to 6.4 percent between 1974 and 1979, and the share claimed by renewable resources climbed from a mere 1.0 percent to 12.0 percent over the same period.[38] (See Table 3.4.)

Yet, in spite of these shifts, even the IEA has suggested that more could be done to change direction. Pointing out that fully three-fourths of the energy R&D expenditures of its member governments are directly concerned with electricity generation, the IEA suggested in a 1980 report that more emphasis should be placed on developing technologies that would directly displace liquid fuels. Moreover, the "important potential contribution" of conservation "still does not appear to be reflected in the level of its funding," the IEA stated.[39]

Table 3.4. Distribution of Energy R&D Expenditures in IEA Member
Countries, 1974–79

| Program | Government funds | | Private funds |
	1974	1979	1979
	(PERCENT)		
Conservation	2.3	6.4	24.5
Renewable resources	1.0	12.0	4.7
Oil and gas	2.2	3.4	21.6
Coal	5.8	10.8	12.4
Nuclear fission	68.7	44.6	15.3*
Nuclear fusion	8.3	10.3	–
Other sources	0.3	0.7	0.9
Supporting technologies	11.1	11.7	20.7
Total**	100.0	100.0	100.0
Total in dollars (billions)	1.9	7.1	2.9

*Includes both fission and fusion.
**May not add to 100 because of rounding.
Source: International Energy Agency

Knowledge for Profits

Defense, space, and basic research programs together account for almost half the total global expenditure on R&D.
They are mostly supported by government funds. The other
half of the global budget is largely financed by private industry,
although there are substantial government investments in such
areas as energy, health, and agriculture.

As already noted, government contracts provide a large share
of the support for R&D in some companies. Close to one-third
of the total research performed in corporate laboratories in
Britain, France, and the United States is supported by government funds. In sharp contrast, in Japan and Switzerland, less
than 2 percent of the R&D performed by corporations is paid
for with tax revenues.[40]

Government support for industrial R&D is heavily concentrated in industries related to defense and space. In the United

States, tax revenues pay for almost 80 percent of the research and development performed by the aerospace industry and nearly half of that carried out by the electrical equipment and telecommunications industries. In France, aerospace companies draw two-thirds and electronics companies about one-third of their research and development funds from the national exchequer.[41]

In contrast, corporations making pharmaceuticals, motor vehicles, and iron and steel perform very little government-sponsored research and development. For such companies, R&D is just like any other business investment—it must be justified in terms of its potential contribution to profits and it must compete with advertising, the purchase of capital equipment, and similar items for its share of corporate funds. In the United States, corporations have plowed an average of about 2 percent of their gross incomes into their research and development laboratories over the past fifteen years, a proportion that falls well short of the share claimed by advertising departments. The proportion varies greatly from industry to industry, however, with the electronics industry investing about 16 percent of its income in R&D and the service industries about 0.3 percent.[42]

Between 1967 and 1975, corporations in Western Europe, North America, and Japan plowed a steadily growing amount of their own funds into laboratories. But government support for industrial R&D during that period fell by almost one-fourth, with much of the decline occurring in the United States as a result of shrinkage in the space program. In the late seventies, U.S. government funding picked up again, with support for energy R&D and increased defense outlays leading the way. These conflicting trends tend to muddy international comparisons of industrial R&D expenditures. Countries such as Japan, in which virtually all industrial R&D is financed by company funds, have seen a steady rise in their total R&D

spending, while countries such as the United States and France have seen rising corporate funding offset by dwindling government support.[43]

Because research and development expenditures derived from company funds provide one measure of the importance attached to innovation by corporate managers, a comparison among industrial countries in the amount of corporate R&D performed per person may provide an indication of relative levels of innovative capacity. According to this measure, the United States still outranks most other industrial countries, although West German and Swedish corporations spend almost as much per person as American corporations do.[44] (See Table 3.5.) Superimposed on these trends is the fact that research and development is highly concentrated in a few companies. In the United States, for example, although more than 10,000 companies perform R&D, just four account for fully 20 percent of the total expenditure and twenty companies together spend about half the total. Indeed, the R&D programs of some companies dwarf those of entire countries.[45]

Table 3.5. Corporate-Funded R&D Per Capita in Selected OECD Countries

Country	1967 Expenditure*	US=100	1975 Expenditure*	US=100
	(US $)		(US $)	
United States	46.7	100	52.1	100
Canada	16.5	35.3	15.2	29.2
France	22.2	47.5	28.4	54.5
West Germany	36.9	79.0	49.1	94.2
Italy	8.6	18.4	11.9	22.8
Japan	22.5	48.1	37.9	72.7
Netherlands	37.6	80.5	36.3	39.7
Sweden	30.3	64.2	50.2	96.4
United Kingdom	36.6	78.4	33.1	63.5

*At 1970 prices and adjusted exchange rates.
Source: Organisation for Economic Cooperation and Development.

(See Table 3.6.)

What is all this money spent on? There is no easy answer, for few governments keep accurate information on the R&D activities of private corporations, and even in those countries where there is a wealth of data—such as the United States—it is not easy to group corporations into well-defined industries. Nevertheless, a rough estimate by the Organisation for Economic Cooperation and Development indicates that in 1975, almost two-thirds of the total industrial R&D in the western industrial countries was performed by three industrial groups: electronics and electrical goods, with 28 percent of the total; chemicals, including the drug industry, with 19 percent; and aerospace with 17 percent. In the United States, six industries—aerospace, electronics, chemicals and drugs, motor vehicles, machinery, and instruments—performed more than four-fifths of the nation's industrial R&D in the late seventies.[46]

Table 3.6. R&D Expenditures by Selected Countries and Corporations, 1975*

Country or corporation	Expenditure
	(MILLIONS OF DOLLARS)
West Germany	8,847
Italy	1,656
Sweden	1,216
General Motors	1,114
International Business Machines	946
Belgium	764
Ford Motor Company	748
American Telephone and Telegraph	619
India	420
Spain	262
International Telephone and Telegraph	219
South Korea	127

*Corporate figures do not include research performed under government contracts. Expenditure calculated at 1975 exchange rates.
Source: Organisation for Economic Corporation and Development, *Business Week*, and U.N. Economic, Social, and Cultural Organization.

While universities are the chief focus for basic research, corporations concentrate on applied research and experimental development. In the United States, less than 3 percent of industrial R&D is devoted to basic research, and this proportion has declined since the late sixties.

The vast majority of industrial R&D is concerned with designing, developing, and testing products—activities such as testing drugs for adverse side-effects, restyling automobile bodies for each year's model change, developing new consumer goods, and so on. It is impossible to estimate precisely how much industrial R&D is directed toward relatively trivial changes to existing products—changes that serve simply to maintain a market edge—but some observers suggest that the proportion is substantial and growing. "There has been recent evidence of a shrinking of time horizons and a growing conservatism regarding industrial R&D," suggests Richard Nelson of Yale University. The reason is that high levels of inflation and economic uncertainty are steering corporations away from exploratory R&D that is likely to have its payoff only in the long term and toward activities designed to maximize short-term profits. Government regulations are also forcing corporations to put more resources into pollution control, energy conservation, and occupational safety and health programs—tasks that require urgent attention.[47]

These massive investments in industrial research and development are thus part of a complex system. On the one hand, the industrial R&D enterprise is driven by the chief corporate objective of increasing profits, and, on the other, by government needs for weapons systems, space vehicles, scientific studies, and other expertise. It is also highly influenced by broad economic factors such as inflation and uncertain prospects for economic growth and by more narrow factors such as government regulations and tax policies. Governments thus have a strong direct influence over industrial research and development because they pay for some of it, and they have an equally strong indirect influence through their general economic and industrial policies.

Needs and Priorities

In spite of the heavy reliance that government officials and corporate leaders place on technology to solve their manifold problems, the distribution of scarce scientific resources is, by any rational measure, seriously distorted with respect to society's real needs.

The priorities reflected in the global research and development budget and the arrangements for funding and performing R&D were essentially laid down in the postwar years, in the corrosive atmosphere of the Cold War and in an era of abundant resources and cheap energy. Now, as the world faces dwindling reserves of oil and gas, rising demands for food and fiber, and deteriorating biological systems, such unproductive tasks as developing more devastating weapons and restyling consumer products still claim the bulk of R&D funds around the world.

Thus, the United States has the ability to survey virtually every square meter of the Soviet Union, yet the world's scientists and engineers have barely begun to survey the complex ecosystems of fast-disappearing tropical rain forests or the malignant spread of the world's deserts. The nuclear arsenals of the superpowers contain enough explosive power to reduce to rubble most of the cities on the globe, yet the more challenging task of providing clean, safe power for those cities has received far less scientific attention.

Driven by the political and commercial motivations of governments and corporations in the industrial world, the global research and development budget is poorly attuned to the needs of the developing countries in general and to the requirements of the poorest people in those countries in particular. Not only does the lack of R&D capacity in Third World countries perpetuate their dependence on imported technology, but it also means that the technologies produced are overwhelmingly geared to the economic environment of the industrial countries—they are capital-intensive, labor-saving, and adapted to large-scale enterprises.

While it is easy to point out the mismatch between the priorities reflected in the world's investment in R&D and its most urgent problems, it is far more difficult to reorder those priorities. When the various actors in the global R&D system perceive a common interest, major new initiatives can be launched with dispatch. The Manhattan Project, which led to the atomic bomb, and the Apollo Project, which culminated in the 1969 moon landing, are the most celebrated examples. But such problems as providing clean and safe energy, reducing poverty, and building sustainable agricultural systems demand actions that cut across a range of vested interests. And unlike building bombs and space vehicles, they involve more than the simple marshalling of science and technology to attain a single objective.

Yet there are many steps that can and should be taken to channel R&D resources into socially productive areas. Governments have considerable flexibility in reordering their own R&D priorities and considerable power to influence the programs of private industry through a combination of incentives and regulations. Universities constitute a major source of scientific and engineering expertise, yet they channel little of this knowledge into the solution of problems in their surrounding communities. In the Third World, R&D institutions are in dire need of aid from the industrial world. And finally, while governments and multinational corporations dominate the funding and performance of R&D, they do not hold a monopoly on human ingenuity; appropriate technology groups in rich and poor countries are developing technologies that have been neglected by major R&D enterprises, but usually such groups are poorly funded and lack official support.

Reordering the world's R&D priorities by channeling more money into neglected programs, new organizations, and Third World laboratories will not be sufficient to solve the world's problems, however. Many tasks are too urgent to wait for R&D to provide solutions and virtually none can be solved by science and technology alone. Indeed, when new knowledge is used to bolster the power of governments, corporations, and ruling elites, it can aggravate the social injustices that lie at the root of many of the world's most urgent problems.

Nevertheless, there are many areas in which R&D can play a key role in determining how society responds to the problems that will present themselves in the decades ahead. The world's research and development program now reflects the needs of the fifties and early sixties. Major changes will be needed to make it more relevant to the eighties and nineties.

4

Innovation, Productivity, and Jobs

The distorted priorities reflected in the global research and development budget help explain why so much technological change is unrelated to the problems confronting the world. But R&D is only one of a constellation of factors that influence the pace and direction of technological innovation.

Innovation, which can loosely be described as the incorporation of new knowledge and ideas into products and processes, is highly susceptible to changing economic and political forces. It also tends to occur in waves, as technological changes in one industry spark innovations in related industries. And, in an increasingly interdependent world economy, technological change is strongly affected by pressures of international economic competition.

The shifting economic tides of the past decade have thus deeply affected patterns of technological innovation. The rate of innovation has slowed down in some sectors and it has picked up in others, and it seems to be occurring more rapidly in some countries than in others. Moreover, there are signs that the world may be in the midst of a transition between two technological periods, for much of the technological change that took place in the fifties and sixties relied heavily on cheap energy and abundant resources.

Two of the most important technologies on the immediate horizon are microelectronics and biotechnology. Both hold immense promise, for they can help overcome energy and resource constraints. But like many other technologies, their widespread use may raise serious problems. They are likely to be at the center of a major restructuring of patterns of production in many sectors in the world economy, which in turn will alter the types of jobs and the skills needed in society. These two technologies help illustrate how innovation, productivity, and jobs are tightly bound together.[1]

An Innovation Recession

The long economic boom that followed World War II was characterized by unprecedented technological change across a broad spectrum of industries. Products changed dramatically as new materials were developed and applied in a wide range of activities; entirely new technologies, such as antibiotic drugs, nuclear energy, and television were introduced; production processes were transformed with the advent of new machine tools and new forms of automation. This surge of innovation was both a contributor to and a result of the transformations that were taking place in the postwar world economy.

One measure of the level of innovation during the fifties and sixties is the sharp rise in productivity that took place throughout the industrial world. Nowhere was this more obvious than in agriculture. Not only did the introduction of labor-saving machinery directly boost output per worker (also displacing millions of farm workers in the process), but the spread of new agricultural technologies also raised crop yields and led to higher levels of production per person. In manufacturing industries, too, the application of new technologies and new forms of industrial organization resulted in sharp increases in output for each hour of labor expended in the factories.

But the unprecedented productivity growth rates achieved during the postwar period began to tail off in many countries in the late sixties, and they went into a slump in the early seventies. The United States and Britain came close to the bottom of the league in productivity growth during the seventies, with growth rates of around 1 percent a year between 1973 and the end of the decade; both countries, in fact, entered the eighties with their productivity levels actually declining. Other industrial countries fared a little better, but as economist Ronald Muller has pointed out, "the American phenomenon is beginning to spread." According to Muller's calculations, if the annual productivity growth rates since 1973 are set against those of the previous decade, Japan's growth rate dropped by 63 percent, West Germany's by 32 percent, France's by 33 percent, Canada's by 75 percent, and Italy's by 80 percent.[2]

Technological change is not the only factor in raising overall levels of productivity. Productivity is generally higher in manufacturing industry than it is in agriculture, and thus part of the reason for the exceptionally high growth rates of the postwar period can be explained by the movement of workers away from the fields into the factories. Part of the slowdown in productivity growth in the seventies is due to the fact that most industrial countries now have a majority of their work force employed in offices and service industries, where tasks are not easy to automate and where productivity consequently increases slowly.

The level of skills in the labor force also affects levels of productivity, since skilled workers generally produce at higher levels. Thus the influx into the workforce of large numbers of relatively unskilled young people and women during the past decade may have reduced rates of productivity growth. Finally, the sharp increase in capital expenditures aimed at controlling pollution and improving safety in the workplace does not register in terms of increased productivity. As Michael Harrington has pointed out, statisticians consider such expenditures as "a diversion of resources from 'productive' uses, including the manufacture of carcinogenic cigarettes. Thus, saving miners' lives in recent years has been a source of 'negative' productivity in the mining industry."[3]

Yet, even when all these factors are taken into account, the steep decline in productivity growth during the seventies remains puzzling. For example, in a survey of trends in the U.S. economy, Edward Denison of the Brookings Institution concluded with refreshing candor that a substantial chunk of the productivity decline defies explanation.[4] A good deal of evidence, however, points to a reduction in the tempo of technological change.

One possible signal of a slowdown in technological innovation is the fact that in many countries there has been a leveling off or even a decline in the number of patents applied for and awarded each year. A survey of patent applications filed between 1963 and 1976 by citizens in nine major industrial countries shows considerable year-to-year fluctuation, but in every country except Japan, the peak year occurred between 1965 and 1970. In the United States, for example, the number of patent applications filed by American citizens dropped from a high of just over 76,000 in 1970 to about 65,000 in 1976. (The total number of patents filed in the United States did not decline so steeply, largely because of an increase in the number of applications filed by noncitizens.) This leveling off is particularly noteworthy since expenditures on industrial research and development continued to expand during the seventies; the productivity of those outlays seems to have declined.[5]

Although these figures are at least suggestive, patent applications show, at best, only a fuzzy outline of innovation trends. Most patents are never put to use, and the overall figures give no indication of trends in the quality of innovative activity, for they make no differentiation between run-of-the-mill inventions and key breakthroughs that launch a major new development. Trends in the number of truly groundbreaking technological advances can only be seen in hindsight, and then usually from a long distance.

An indication of a slowdown in the number of major advances—or at least in their commercial application—can be seen in the trends in the number of new companies started up during the seventies, however. New companies, particularly in the United States, have been the source of a disporportionate amount of groundbreaking technological innovation. Frequently started with a few hundred thousand dollars of venture capital as seed money, and often based on one or two key patents, small, high-technology companies have pioneered in the development of several important new technologies. Polaroid and Xerox were launched in this manner, for example, and most of the important developments in microelectronics were carried out by small firms established in the United States in the sixties.

The typical life cycle of a new company proceeds through a start-up phase, in which seed money provides the basis for early growth, to the point at which shares are sold to the public in order to generate new investment capital. The number of new companies that sell shares for the first time—"go public" in Wall Street parlance—thus provides an indication of the level of activity in this important area of the economy and gives a measure of the financial interest in supporting new ventures. In 1969, more than 1,000 companies went public in the United States, and two years later, even though the economy was going through a difficult period, 646 companies raised more than $3.3 billion on the stock exchange when they sold shares for the first time. But a slump set in in 1974, and during the next four years only a handful of new companies went public.[6]

Not all of the companies spawned in the boom years of the late sixties and early seventies were based on the latest technology. But a study conducted by the Department of Commerce shows how deeply the slump affected small, high-technology ventures. In 1969, some 204 technology-based companies went public, but the number dropped to just four in 1974. Part of the reason for this decline was a drought in venture capital, the seed money that provides the initial support for many new companies. Between 1970 and 1977, the venture capital business was "practically dead," reported *Business Week*. In the late seventies and early eighties, however, there were signs of new life in venture capital markets and in the subsequent public launching of new companies. The resurgence was barely dented by the recession that struck the American economy in that period.[7]

There were thus several disparate indications of a slowdown in technological advance during the seventies. The appearance of an innovation recession is, however, easier to discern than are the causes. Part of the explanation lies in the general state of the world economy. The persistence of sluggish economic growth and limited increases in productivity have resulted in a vicious cycle: technological innovation is needed to raise growth rates, but industry is reluctant, or unable, to invest in new technology during a recession. Labor-saving technological change—the basis of much of the productivity surge of the postwar period—is also more vigorously resisted when unemployment is high and displaced workers have few alternative employment possibilities.

The vicious cycle of slow growth and lagging innovation is particularly evident in industries such as steel and automobile manufacturing, where international competition has heated up while sales have stagnated. A 1980 study of technological trends in the steel industry, conducted by the Congressional Office of Technology Assessment (OTA), concluded that American steel manufacturers must spend at least $3 billion a year in the early eighties to modernize their plants. This level of expenditure will be needed if the U.S. steel industry is to hold its own against imports from technologically more advanced plants in Japan, West Germany, and some Third World countries, OTA suggested. Such a modernization program will require annual investments at least 50 percent higher than the industry made in the late seventies, and these outlays will have to be made at a time when sales and profitability are expected to be low because of sluggish world demand. The alternative, however, is a continued loss of market share and a further decline in profits. A similar dismal choice faces steelmakers in many other countries where failure to invest in new technologies during the seventies has made their plants relatively unproductive.[8]

The problems facing the automobile industry are similar. American car manufacturers are now in the midst of an $80 billion retooling program aimed at producing more fuel-efficient cars, at a time when they are reporting record losses. Again, they have no alternative but to transform obsolete products that are no match for technologically more sophisticated imports. Some automobile manufacturers in other countries are also faced with the necessity of revamping and automating their production lines in order to compete effectively with manufacturers who have raised productivity through labor-saving automation. Like the steel industry, the problems facing automobile manufacturers stem partly from lack of innovation in the seventies and the failure to anticipate the impact of sharply increased oil prices.

The difficulties facing the steel and automobile industries are matched in many sectors where growth is sluggish and demand is depressed. A report by the Organisation for Economic Cooperation and Development describes how these economic conditions affect technological change over the long term: "Slack capacity and diminished expectations regarding future demands damp down investments in new plant and equipment, reducing the growth of physical capital per employed worker and diminishing the pace at which new technologies are brought into practice. Over the still longer run, R&D incentives themselves are damped." The study concludes that "there is evidence that all of these reactions have occurred and are occurring."[9]

Technological Change and Business Cycles

If sluggish growth and dampened demand alone were responsible for the slowdown in innovation, an economic upturn should bring forth a new surge of technological advance. But the innovation recession of the past decade may actually represent a transition between two distinct technological periods. For one thing, many of the technologies introduced in the fifties and sixties relied heavily on the availability of cheap energy. And for another, the wave of innovation that followed World War II may simply have run its economic course and a new wave of very different innovations may be gathering to take its place.

The idea that major technological innovations are often clumped together and that they coincide with periods of rapid economic growth was put forward in 1939 by the economist Joseph Schumpeter to explain the reason for long-term cycles of economic activity in the industrial countries. The existence of such cycles had been described a decade earlier by the Soviet economist Kondratiev, who pointed out that business activity occurred in waves, which took between forty and sixty years to rise and fall. Schumpeter argued that technological innovations resulting from the development of steam power provided the driving force behind the first Kondratiev wave in the late eighteenth and early nineteenth centuries; the development of railroads and associated technologies in the late nineteenth century undergirded the second Kondratiev wave; and innovations related to electric power and the internal combustion engine drove the third Kondratiev wave in the first half of the twentieth century.

Although this explanation for cycles of economic growth ignores the influence of changing economic and social forces on the processes of technological change itself, it is clear that periods of rapid economic growth are frequently associated with a cluster of groundbreaking technological innovations. Such was the case in the postwar period, when technological advances in a broad range of industries spread rapidly throughout the economy as innovations in one industry were taken up and exploited by allied industries. Many of these innovations resulted from the accumulation of knowledge and the development of new technologies in the war years and from the rapid buildup of research and development immediately following the war. The chemical and petrochemical industries are a prime example of this process.

Advances in chemistry and in petroleum refining from the thirties on laid the basis for an astonishing variety of new materials, ranging from synthetic fibers to new plastics and synthetic rubber. These materials in turn helped to transform allied industries, such as textiles, construction, and automobile manufacturing, as the chemical innovations spread throughout the economy. At the same time, a combination of new knowledge in chemistry and biology resulted in the production of an array of drugs that in turn brought under control a host of infectious diseases that had dogged humanity for centuries. And a marriage between chemistry and metallurgy spawned a range of new alloys that underpinned developments in the aerospace, energy, machine tools, and similar industries.

By the late sixties, however, there were signs that this postwar wave of innovations was beginning to die down. In synthetic fiber production, for example, the surge of new products that began with the introduction of nylon in 1939 and which saw a range of new materials developed in the fifties and sixties, slowed and changed direction in the seventies. Virtually no radically new synthetic fiber has been introduced in the past decade, and the industry has turned its attention toward incremental improvements in production technology. This trend is not limited solely to fiber production. A 1979 survey of the chemical industry by the *Economist* reported that "technology has reached a plateau. The pioneering days of knitting new molecular combinations for big new plastics and fibers are over. Only the more difficult molecular chains are left to be worked on, and the promise of high returns has faded."[10] This innovation slowdown, it should be noted, has occurred in spite of increased expenditures on research and development in these industries.

Agriculture shows a similar pattern of rapid technological advance and sharp increases in productivity during the quarter-century following World War II, but of more limited innovation in the seventies. As Lester Brown has pointed out, "From the beginning of agriculture until World War II, land productivity increased very slowly. For long periods of time, it did not increase at all. Rice yields in Japan during the nineteenth century were only marginally higher than those during the fourteenth century. Corn yields in the United States during the thirties were the same as those during the 1860s, the first decade for which reliable yield estimates are available. Following World War II, however, crop yields began to rise rapidly in virtually every industrial country."[11]

Worldwide, the amount of cereals produced per acre climbed by about 2.4 percent a year throughout the fifties and sixties, and in the United States, it rose by a spectacular 4.0 percent a year in that period. Behind these trends lay a variety of technological innovations, ranging from the development of new processes for making nitrogen fertilizer cheaply from natural gas feedstocks to the introduction of a host of new pesticides and herbicides. In addition, the development of new plant breeding techniques in the sixties led to the spread of varieties of crop plants that were particularly responsive to increased fertilizer use—the so-called Green Revolution varieties.[12]

Since the early seventies, however, yields have grown more slowly and they have become more erratic. Countries as diverse as the United States, France, Egypt, and China experienced a slowdown in the growth of productivity of their agricultural lands in the seventies. Although the reasons for this break in the postwar trend differ from country to country, such factors as the increasing use of more marginal land, the sharp rise in fertilizer prices resulting from the oil-price hikes, and poor weather in the early seventies were significant in each case. But there were also signs that the surge in innovation had begun to die down.

Following the initial successes in plant breeding in the sixties, new varieties introduced during the seventies showed less dramatic yield increases. There were also some frustrations, such as difficulties in breeding varieties of corn with high lysine content and the inability to repeat with soybeans the yield improvements achieved with cereal crops. Problems also began to appear with many pesticides, as signs of environmental contamination became too obvious to ignore and as many pests developed resistance to the compounds introduced in the previous decades. Since the early seventies, few effective new pesticides have been introduced.[13]

More direct evidence of a slowdown in technological advance has been reported by Louis Thompson, associate dean of agriculture at Iowa State University, and Neal Jensen, professor of plant breeding at Cornell University. Thompson has noted that in the late fifties, there was a wide gap in the yields achieved on experimental plots and those achieved on average farms in Iowa, but by the early seventies, this gap had virtually disappeared. In effect, the backlog of technology available to farmers in Iowa had largely been used up. Jensen arrived at a similar conclusion from studies of wheat yields in New York State. He suggested, in an article published in *Science* magazine, that "the rate of productivity increase will become slower and will eventually become level." Jensen also suggests that plant breeders in the advanced industrial countries have already raised yields almost as far as they can.[14]

These trends in the chemical industry and in agriculture do not mean that the spectacular wave of innovation during the postwar period has fizzled out entirely. The developments of the past decade reflect a typical maturing process in which rapid change takes place in the early years as new innovations are exploited, but the pace of change slows down as the innovations run their course and as attention turns to incremental improvements in existing technologies. Jay Forrester, professor of management at Massachusetts Institute of Technology, puts the argument succinctly: "Our present technology is mature. Since 1960 there has not been a major, radically new, commercially successful technological innovation comparable to aircraft, television, nylon, antibiotics, computers, or solid-state electronics. The things that are truly new do not fit into the present technological infrastructure: they must wait until the next great technological wave. . . . We are nearing the end of a technological era."[15]

It is not necessary to take such an apocalyptic view to realize that fundamental shifts in the patterns of innovation are under way. Innovation has not died down in all industries; indeed, it is accelerating in some sectors of the economy. Leading the way is the development and application of microelectronics, a technology that began to flower in the seventies. And more recent developments in the biological sciences also promise to spark off a surge of innovation in the eighties and beyond. If the theory of Kondratiev waves of innovation is correct, these technologies are likely to be the leaders of technological and innovative growth in the eighties.

Just as advances in chemistry and materials technology sparked technological changes in a broad range of industries in the postwar era, microelectronics and biotechnology will have a pervasive impact in the decades ahead. As these technologies are developed and applied, they will lead to fundamental changes in industrial production and in the organization of work and daily lives. Moreover, unlike most of the technologies that underpinned the postwar wave of innovation, microelectronics and biotechnology do not require the use of large amounts of energy and material resources. The evolution and potential use of these technologies illustrate many of the key issues surrounding technological change, productivity, and jobs.

The Microelectronics Revolution

It is time to sit up and take notice when a committee of the National Academy of Sciences states that "the modern era of electronics has ushered in a second industrial revolution . . . its impact on society could be even greater than that of the original industrial revolution." Academy committees are not usually noted for hyperbole.[16]

The Academy is not alone in suggesting that recent advances in electronic technology are harbingers of sweeping social changes. In the past decade, when most industries experienced sluggish growth and flagging innovation, the electronics industry saw its sales boom and its products change dramatically. The key to these developments is the ability to imprint tens of thousands of electronic components and complex circuits on chips of silicon one-fourth the size of a postage stamp. This technological feat has shrunk the size of electronic equipment, increased the power and flexibility of small computers, and slashed the cost of storing and manipulating information. It also promises to revolutionize patterns of industrial production and lead to increased levels of automation in factories and offices.[17]

The development of this new microelectronic technology is being spurred by massive investments from governments and corporations around the world. Indeed, the pressure of international competition has become one of the chief driving forces behind the swift pace of change in microelectronics. The economic stakes are high. By the end of the eighties, the electronics industry is expected to rival the automobile, steel, and chemical industries in economic importance. Indeed, Arthur Robinson, writing in *Science* magazine, has suggested that "if steel and oil have been two of the key ingredients of modern industrial society up to now, many believe that in the remainder of this century it will be the state of a nation's electronics industry that signifies whether it is a developed nation or not."[18]

The technological advances that have propelled the electronics industry into the front ranks of the world's leading economic sectors began in the late forties with the development of the transistor. But the pace of change quickened dramatically in the seventies as new techniques led to stunning levels of miniaturization in electronic components. By the end of the decade, electronic circuitry that once would have filled a room could be etched on a silicon chip measuring just five millimeters across; the most densely packed chips, known as integrated circuits, contained close to 100,000 electronic components. It is expected that by the late eighties, at least one million components will be crammed onto a single silicon chip.

These developments, furthermore, have slashed the cost of electronic equipment because once a particular integrated circuit is designed and tested, it can be mass produced at relatively low cost. This means that an electronic circuit that just a few years ago would have been built by the expensive and laborious process of wiring together thousands of individual parts, can now be bought off the shelf for a few dollars.

Most integrated circuits are designed for specific tasks, such as operating a digital watch or storing information in a computer memory. In 1971, however, the American microelectronics company Intel brought out a radically different, more flexible type of integrated circuit that vastly extended the range of applications of microelectronic technology. Intel essentially put the entire central processing unit of a computer—the complex circuitry that processes information and carries out computations—on a silicon chip. The resulting integrated circuit, known as a microprocessor, can be programmed like a computer to carry out a broad range of functions.

The central processing units of powerful computers that would have cost thousands of dollars to produce a few years ago are being mass-produced today for a few dollars apiece. A startling achievement in its own right, this development means that the computer's ability to process information and carry out instructions can now be incorporated relatively cheaply into a variety of machines, ranging from cruise missiles to microwave ovens.

These tiny electronic devices did not emerge suddenly from the laboratory bench and begin to change society, however. As with any new technology, the development of microelectronics has been pulled along by economic and political forces. During the sixties, the U.S. military and space programs provided the driving force, accounting for most of the integrated circuits produced in the United States. This burgeoning military demand provided a stable market for the small, innovative microelectronics companies that spearheaded the technological development, and it helped launch the industry on its high-growth trajectory.[19] It also changed the nature of many weapons. Microelectronic controls now constitute the brains of guided missiles, "smart" bombs, electronic sensors, and other ingredients of modern warfare, and have played a central role in the development of military space systems.

During the seventies, the focus shifted toward civilian applications, and commercial incentives are now pushing the development of the technology. The manufacture of integrated circuits has turned into a $10-billion-a-year industry, and sales have been growing at the phenomenal rate of 30 percent per year. Military programs account for about $1 billion worth of microelectronic devices, and the rest of the expenditure is widely disseminated throughout the economy.[20]

The biggest single user of microelectronics is the computer industry itself. The development of cheap and powerful microprocessors and integrated memory circuits has spawned a broad range of small, flexible computers that can be programmed for a variety of tasks. Just a few years ago, the cheapest computers on the market cost hundreds of thousands of dollars and they were big, powerful machines. Now home computers the size of a typewriter can be bought for less than $1,000, and powerful business machines for less than $10,000. These developments have brought computing power to the fingertips of a rapidly growing number of people. They have also opened the way for the widespread use of computers to control industrial machinery and for an expansion of electronic record-keeping, information processing, and data gathering.

Although for many people the chief manifestation of this microelectronics revolution is the transformation that has taken place in many consumer goods and gadgets—the manufacture of pocket calculators, digital watches, and electronic toys and games mushroomed into a $4-billion-a-year business in the late seventies—it is in the workplace that the new technology will ultimately have its chief social impact. Electronic machinery is already beginning to change jobs in establishments as diverse as banks and steelworks. No technology in history has had such a broad range of applications in the workplace.[21]

The spreading use of computer-controlled machinery in factory production is leading to new levels and forms of automation. In giant industrial plants such as oil refineries, power stations, chemical factories, and steelworks, small computers and microprocessors built directly into measuring instruments are being used to control temperatures, pressures, and the flow of materials. These tasks are, however, already highly automated, and the use of microelectronics will essentially allow more precise control over plant operations. In many other factories, microelectronic devices will extend computer controls to tasks that have previously remained relatively immune to automation. Indeed, it is in the machine shops and on the assembly lines of manufacturing industries that microelectronics will ultimately have its chief industrial impact.[22]

The key to the growing use of electronics on the factory floor lies in the ability to incorporate microprocessor controls directly into machinery such as lathes, grinders, and cutting machines. These computer-controlled machine tools operate according to sets of programmed instructions, and by simply changing the programs, they can swiftly be made to shift from one task to another. This flexibility is of fundamental importance. Until now, automation has been largely restricted to factories that turn out thousands of identical products, because it has been too costly to retool machines at frequent intervals to perform new tasks. But the development of reprogrammable machinery makes it economically feasible to automate production processes that involve short production-runs and frequent changes in machine settings. The majority of manufacturing processes fall into this category.[23]

Computer-based automation is also being extended to the assembly stage of production. A new generation of microelectronically controlled robots is being developed to perform a wide range of complex tasks on assembly lines. These machines bear little resemblance to the androids of the film *Star Wars*. They consist of a flexible arm, with two or more joints that are controlled automatically, on the end of which is a tool such as a drill or a paint spray. Some of the more advanced robots can be reprogrammed by typing new instructions on a keyboard or by inserting a new magnetic disk into the machine. A computer-controlled welding machine, for example, can weld a Ford Pinto one minute and a Mustang the next. The automobile industry is leading the way in the use of robots. For example, in Nissan's Zama plant near Tokyo, 96 percent of the welding is done by robots, a level that is being matched in some of the newest plants in Europe and the United States. By 1987, 90 percent of the new machines bought by General Motors will be computer-controlled, predicts G.M. president E. M. Estes.[24]

Although the use of robots is increasing rapidly, most of the current generation of machines are limited to relatively simple, routine tasks. But as the technology becomes more sophisticated, robots will become more versatile and their potential uses will multiply. The key step in this development will be to equip robots with a sense of vision by using powerful microprocessors and computer memory to link the image produced by a camera with the machine's actions. Such robots are already under development, and prototype production lines employing "seeing" robots have been set up in the United States and Japan. Parallel development efforts aimed at equipping robots with sensitive pads that would enable them to discern objects by a sense of "touch" are also well along in several laboratories.[25]

The development of this new generation of more intelligent robots will greatly extend the number of jobs that machines can perform, for they would be used to carry out more intricate tasks than today's robots can tackle. For example, a Fiat executive suggested to *Business Week* that with sensory robots it would be possible to reduce the number of workers required in some plants to about 10 percent of current levels.[26]

Robots are not cheap. The current generation of machines starts at around $35,000 for a model that can be programmed to carry out several tasks. One equipped with vision or touch sensors would cost at least $75,000. But even at these prices, robots can represent an attractive economic proposition. According to Joe Engelberger, president of a large American robot company, an average robot costs about $4.80 per hour to operate when it is used for sixteen hours per day. That is less than half the wage earned by a worker on an assembly line. As the market expands and the cost of microelectronic controls continues to drop, the price of robots is expected to decline. This trend will be greatly accelerated if some of the major electronics companies enter the business, for manufacturing costs are likely to go down as production volume rises. According to a projection by a leading Wall Street investment analyst, as many as 200,000 robots per year could be sold in the U.S. by the end of the eighties if the major computer makers enter the business.[27]

The growing sophistication and flexibility of microelectronically-controlled machine tools and robots means that a large range of jobs can be automated. But the ultimate impact of these machines will extend well beyond the piecemeal automation of individual tasks, for it is now possible to devise a factory in which computer-controlled equipment carries out an entire production operation.

In such a plant, a large central computer guides the operations of minicomputers and microprocessors that in turn control the operations of machine tools and robots. The design of parts and of finished products is carried out with the aid of a computer, which then generates a program to control the machine tool that will manufacture the product. As the European Trade Union Institute tersely notes, "the highly skilled toolmaker's job is thereby completely eliminated."[28]

Although such a plant sounds like something dreamed up by science-fiction writers, it may not be too far away. The production of integrated circuits, for example, incorporates some of these features, for computer-generated circuit designs are transferred onto masks that govern the automated manufacturing process. The U.S. Air Force is also coordinating a program in which about eighty aerospace companies are attempting to apply computer-aided design and manufacturing techniques to the production of aircraft and missiles. And in Japan, the Ministry of Trade and Industry is sponsoring an effort to develop a completely automated production facility by 1985.[29]

The application of microelectronics in the workplace will not stop at the factory gate. Office work is also in the midst of fundamental change as computerized equipment is being developed to speed up and automate many tasks. The incentive to automate office work is obvious enough. Although office employment has been increasing rapidly in recent decades, the productivity of office workers has remained relatively static. According to one estimate, while the productivity of office workers rose by about 4 percent between 1960 and 1970, that of blue-collar workers almost doubled. The reason is simple: factory workers are backed by increasingly sophisticated technologies, yet most office workers rely on equipment and technologies that have changed little in fifty years.[30]

The average factory worker operates about $25,000 worth of machinery, while the average office worker uses less than $2,000 worth of typewriters, filing cabinets, copiers, and other equipment. But the rapid proliferation of smart machines, such as small computers, word processors, facsimile machines, and computerized telephone terminals, is beginning to change this pattern of expenditure.

Consider, for example, the recent surge in sales of small computers and their use in a broadening array of offices. The Electronic Industries Association (EIA), an American trade organization, has reported that some 138,000 minicomputers —defined as machines priced from $5,000 to $40,000—were sold in the United States in 1979 alone. By 1984, the association predicts, sales could nearly triple, to 382,000 machines per year. Another study reported by EIA found that the sales of computers priced below $10,000 apiece, which includes home computers as well as business machines, climbed from $276 million in 1978 to $658 million in 1979 and are headed toward a projected $2.4 billion in 1984. Just a decade ago, there were reckoned to be less than 100,000 computers in use worldwide. Sales of word processors have also mushroomed in the past few years. In 1978, there were estimated to be 100,000 word processors in Europe and 400,000 in the United States. In 1980, U.S. sales alone are expected to climb past $1 billion—more than 100,000 separate machines—and a $2-billion-per-year market is expected to develop by 1983.[31]

All of this technological wizardry is being pushed along by some of the biggest names in the corporate world. IBM, Xerox, and even Exxon are developing complete lines of office equipment in the United States; in Europe, such industrial giants as Siemens and Philips have joined the fray; and in Japan, giant electronic conglomerates such as Hitachi are pursuing the technology. Scores of smaller firms are also producing electronic office equipment, computers, and peripheral devices that can be linked to existing machines. It should be noted that all this activity has blossomed since microelectronics came of age less than a decade ago.

These new business machines on their own can increase the efficiency with which some office tasks are carried out. But the full impact of this flood of office technology will only be felt when the machines are linked in far-flung networks through which information can be transported, stored, and processed. This potential merger of computing, word processing, and telecommunications is at the heart of the much-touted information revolution.

In theory, for example, it is possible to transmit information between word processors, computers, facsimile machines, and so on through the telephone system, bypassing the cumbersome and paper-clogged mails. Electronic cash registers—close cousins to small computers and word processors—can be hooked up to bank computers to debit a customer's account directly, eliminating the need for checks or cash. They can also record sales of individual items and relay the information to a central computer that looks after stock control. And computers, word processors, and even modified domestic television sets can be linked to electronic data banks to receive information electronically "without the services of filing, library, and secretarial staff," the European Trade Union Institute laconically notes.[32]

The expanded use of electronic business machines also suggests that there will be sweeping changes in the way that some offices are structured, with work increasingly being diverted to the new machinery, some jobs being eliminated, and other jobs being reclassified. All this is likely to cause major upheavals and changes in working conditions. As a report by Working Women, an American association of office workers, points out, "because the new technology is being developed to computerize the very flow of work in the office, its potential impact is qualitatively different from previous office equipment which 'mechanized' or 'automated' routine tasks."[33]

In many respects, the development and application of microelectronics brings into focus the issues that surround the so-called reindustrialization policies being pursued by several western governments. At the heart of those policies is an attempt to boost productivity by stimulating high-technology industries that offer prospects for rapid growth and long-term economic success. Since the electronics industry is one of the leading growth areas in an otherwise flaccid global economy, it has naturally risen to the forefront of discussions of reindustrialization. The hope is that microelectronics will be able to overcome some of the constraints on productivity growth that have emerged in virtually every country in recent years. Indeed, the Organisation for Economic Cooperation and Development has suggested that "the electronics complex will be the main pole around which the productive structures of advanced industrial societies will be reorganised."[34]

In part, the attention being lavished on microelectronics—and the government funds being poured into its development—is a response to international economic pressures. In an interdependent world economy, governments have little choice but to ensure that their high-technology industries are in good health. As a 1978 paper by Britain's Labour government put it, "As a trading nation we have only one realistic option—to seize the opportunity provided by this new technology to catch up with our industrial competitors and to adopt and develop it at least as fast and as comprehensively as they do. To opt out will lead to the very worst fears being realised." A report to the French government put the matter a little more starkly: "France is being forced by the imperative of foreign trade to compete in a race over which it has no control."[35]

There are two dimensions to this international race. The first is the competition to stay in the vanguard of the technology behind the construction of integrated circuits. And the second is the competition to use microelectronics in goods and industrial processes in order to boost productivity.

The benefits of keeping abreast of the technology are in one sense obvious—there is a $10 billion global market in microelectronic components; but there are also hidden advantages in the cross-fertilization between designers and users of microelectronics. The United States has long dominated the development and marketing of microelectronic technology. Virtually all the early innovations were made in the U.S. by a handful of companies that were established in the sixties with a few million dollars of venture capital apiece. These initial investments have since been turned into annual turnovers of hundreds of millions of dollars. These small innovative companies eclipsed the big electronics conglomerates such as RCA and Westinghouse by moving rapidly into the commercial production of each new technological breakthrough. Today, the bulk of integrated circuits produced in the United States is still made by semiconductor companies that specialize in the manufacture of microelectronic components and market them to manufacturers of electronic equipment. In the past few years, however, several of these companies have been taken over by large corporations that have come up with the capital needed to finance the costly expansion of production lines.[36]

United States companies held about 70 percent of the world market for microelectronics components in 1979, but rapid technological advances by Japanese companies are beginning to threaten American hegemony in some areas. The Japanese recognized in the early seventies that microelectronics and computer technology would be a cornerstone of industrial progress in the coming decades, and a government-sponsored effort was launched to foster a domestic microelectronics industry. This effort has met with considerable success in several areas. Japanese companies in the late seventies produced about 40 percent of the world market for the most sophisticated computer-memory circuit, and they launched the next generation of memory chips at the same time as their American competitors. In this area, they are now regarded as being at least on a par with companies in the United States.[37]

While American and Japanese firms have been racing ahead with development of the technology, European microelectronics has been lagging. European companies produced less than one-third of the integrated circuits used by European industry, and they are expected to remain dependent on American and Japanese suppliers for some time to come. Several European governments have, however, recently taken steps to foster domestic microelectronics development. These include the establishment in Britain of a company called Inmos, with $120 million of public funds to produce state-of-the-art integrated circuits.[38]

As for the race to incorporate microelectronic technology

into products and processes, again, the United States holds a lead but Japan is moving up fast. American companies use about half of the integrated circuits produced worldwide, which is partly a reflection of the fact that American computer companies—the largest users of microelectronics—have a commanding position in the world market. In other areas too, such as consumer electronics, industrial control equipment, and office machinery, American companies have moved rapidly to incorporate microelectronics into their products.

But, according to a report by the Organisation for Economic Cooperation and Development, "Japan is undoubtedly the country with the most consistent medium- and long-term programme for industrial electronics, ranging from components through automated control systems, to capital goods." Japan already boasts at least half the world's working robots, and a vigorous program supported by the Ministry of International Trade and Industry is racing to develop new industrial automation techniques.[39]

European governments are also sponsoring ambitious programs to encourage their domestic industries to adopt new microelectronic technologies. According to one estimate, all told, European governments have launched programs that will entail expenditures of about $1 billion to stimulate the domestic production and use of microelectronics.[40]

International economic competition is thus working strongly to push the development and application of this new technology. During the next few decades, it will become pervasive, and its social impacts are likely to be equally far-reaching.

Biotechnology: A New Source of Growth?

October 14, 1980 was a historic day on Wall Street. A small genetic engineering company called Genentech, which had yet to put a product on the market, broke all records when it offered its stock to the public for the first time. The price per share soared from \$35 to \$89 in a matter of minutes, making it the hottest new company to go public for decades. It was, according to the *Wall Street Journal,* "the most striking price explosion of a new stock within memory of most stockbrokers."[41]

This intense financial interest in genetic engineering reflects the extraordinary promise of a rash of biological technologies that have been developed over the past few years. Collectively known as biotechnology, the new field, according to its boosters, could lead to improvements in agricultural productivity, novel ways to manufacture chemicals and drugs, and new routes to the development of renewable energy resources. If the promises become reality, biotechnology could be every bit as sweeping in its economic and social impacts as microelectronics. That, at least, is the feeling of the Commission of the European Communities, which suggested in a recent study that "biotechnology could establish itself as the driving force of new-found growth over the coming decades."[42]

So far, much of the biotechnology boom remains a matter of speculation, but the development of the technology today resembles that of microelectronics a decade ago. Genentech and a handful of other small companies, established with venture capital as seed money, are pioneering in the development of biotechnology. It is also attracting attention and cash from some of the world's largest corporations, including Standard Oil of California, Hoechst, the International Nickel Company, Imperial Chemical Industries, DuPont, Monsanto, Aetna Insurance, and Lubrizol. In addition, the British and French governments have launched biotechnology companies with injections of public funds. This immense industrial might is pushing the technology along at an astonishing pace.[43]

Biotechnology encompasses many things. In broad terms, it is the use of organisms and cells to produce a variety of products and to carry out a broad range of tasks. It is not exactly novel: people have been using biotechnology for centuries in the making of leavened bread and in the fermentation of vegetable matter to produce beer, wine, and other alcoholic beverages. And in the past few decades, microorganisms have been put to increasing use in such areas as sewage treatment and the production of antibiotic drugs. But some key scientific advances in the early seventies have laid the basis for a vast expansion of biotechnology. In essence, these advances permit scientists to manipulate cells and organisms in a precise manner, causing them to manufacture substances that they would not normally produce and enhancing their capacity to perform important biological functions.

Just as the history of microelectronics can be traced back three decades to the development of the transistor, the new biotechnology stems from the discovery in 1953 of the nature of DNA, the immensely complex molecules that contain an organism's genetic program. Building upon this discovery, advances in genetics and allied biological sciences have led to a deeper understanding of the functioning of living things. In 1973, two decades after the structure of DNA was worked out, scientists at Stanford University and the University of California developed a powerful technique for manipulating this genetic material. The technique is the key to many of the potential applications of biotechnology.

In essence, the technique, known as recombinant DNA or gene splicing, enables scientists to take genes from one organism and splice them into the DNA of another. Among other things, this may permit human genes that govern the natural production in the body of compounds such as insulin, interferon, and growth hormone to be incorporated into bacteria, which would then be induced to manufacture the compound. In effect, the genetically engineered bacteria would become tiny, living, chemical factories.

There are, however, delicate scientific problems involved in this procedure. As science writer Nicholas Wade explains, "Though the technique was invented seven years ago, biologists are only now working out the nuts and bolts of a commercially viable process. The gene of interest, that for human interferon, say, has first to be fished out of a cell possessing some 100,000 other genes. Other sequences of DNA must be attached to it which signal the bacterium's protein-making machinery to manufacture the gene's product in commercially significant quantities."[44]

Nevertheless, many of the problems have been overcome and it is expected that several companies will be marketing bacterially-produced insulin and interferon in the early eighties. Both are likely to be big money-spinners. Insulin is extremely difficult and expensive to produce by conventional means, and the bacterial route to its production offers a cheaper and simpler alternative. Inteferon, a compound that destroys viruses and which may have a role in cancer therapy, is predicted to have a potential market of about $3 billion by the mid-eighties.[45]

Lucrative though these applications of genetic engineering may be, they represent only a tiny fraction of the potential fruits of this new technology. Using gene splicing and other biological techniques developed in the past few years, scientists are working on novel approaches to the production of vaccines against diseases such as malaria, hepatitis, and hoof and mouth disease. Research into these areas is already well along in several university laboratories and the commercial potential has not been lost on some of the small genetic engineering companies, which are also pursuing the technologies.

Although these applications of biotechnology have received most of the attention, developments outside the pharmaceutical industry are likely to be more far reaching. As a chemical trade publication has noted, "The revolution in applied biology . . . has spread far beyond drugmaking. It is advancing into agriculture, forestry, energy, chemical feedstocks, and other areas that provide the chemical process industries with materials or markets."[46]

The production of alcohol fuels from biomass is one area that is receiving a good deal of attention from several commercial enterprises. Ethanol is currently produced in an age-old process in which yeast is used to break down sugars derived from plant materials. Crops such as sugar cane, sugar beets, and sweet sorghum yield fermentable sugars when they are crushed, but starchy products such as corn and cassava must first be heated and treated with acids and enzymes before they can be fermented, a process that increases costs and requires energy. However, research at several universities and some commercial enterprises is attempting to produce yeast strains that will be able to convert starch directly into alcohol. Another project, under way at the Genex Corporation, a small biotechnology company in Maryland, is aimed at the development of a microorganism that will convert sugar to alcohol at high temperatures, which would enable the alcohol to be distilled off as soon as it is manufactured. Although some of these processes involve formidable problems that have yet to be worked out, they are far from being consigned to the distant realm of science fiction: in October 1980, the National Distillers and Chemical Corporation announced plans to construct a $100 million facility to produce fuel alcohol using genetically engineered yeast strains developed by the Cetus Corporation in Berkeley, California.[47]

As well as producing energy from renewable resources, biotechnology may also lead to substantial energy savings in the production of chemicals and other industrial products. Leslie Glick, president of Genex, has pinpointed a range of organic chemicals, worth more than $12 billion in 1979 prices, which he believes are likely to be produced by genetically engineered bacteria in the relatively near future using processes that are cheaper and less energy-intensive than traditional production methods. Cetus, for example, has been negotiating with Standard Oil of California to begin a joint venture aimed at using biotechnology techniques to produce major building blocks for petrochemicals and synthetic materials. The new process would work at room temperature and low pressures instead of the high temperatures and pressures now employed in the manufacture of these chemicals. Peter Farley, president of Cetus, has suggested that the new process will be "the first substantive case where microbiology will take a shot at the heart of the chemical industry."[48]

It is in agriculture, however, that biotechnology will probably have its most important impacts. An official at the U.S. Department of Agriculture has called the new biotechnology "one of the most important areas for the growth of agriculture, if not the most important in the long term."[49] Engineering crop plants to produce higher yields is as old as agriculture itself. Farmers have always chosen seeds from their best plants for the following year's crop, a process that selects the desirable genetic strains. But in the past few decades, these time-honored techniques have been greatly extended by the development of new plant-breeding methods that have resulted in the production of higher-yielding and disease-resistant varieties. For example, the development of new rice strains, by crossbreeding dwarf varieties with high-yielding plants, resulted in a short, productive plant that does not fall over when the grain matures. This is the basis of the Green Revolution in much of Asia.

These plant-breeding techniques are slow and cumbersome, however. It can take many years to crossbreed different varieties, grow them to maturity, and test them for resistance to plant diseases. But in recent years, scientists have begun to carry out some of the breeding steps in test tubes and petri dishes, using techniques that may eventually speed up breeding processes and permit more precise selection of promising strains. The basis of these new techniques is a method of growing entire plants from single cells or even from protoplasts, cells whose walls have been chemically removed.

These methods, known as tissue culture, result in genetically identical plants that can easily be screened for disease resistance, adaptability to different soils, and so on. Already, Unilever, a multinational agribusiness corporation, has grown oil palms from cells taken from a particularly productive, disease-resistant plant and is testing them on a plantation in Malaysia. In the same way, disease-resistant potato varieties have been grown from plant protoplasts. Hugh Bollinger, a plant scientist who co-founded a small biotechnology company in Utah, has called tissue culture "the botanical equivalent of the laser, in that there are more potential applications than originally conceived." In particular, he notes, the technique can be used for growing thousands of copies of endangered plant species—it has already been applied to a species of cactus that had almost become extinct in the United States—and it may offer a way to bring little-known plant species into rapid agricultural use. "In a fraction of the time required to implement traditional breeding programs," Bollinger notes, "plant materials can be produced and dispersed to other farmers for planting or to other nations for further research and development."[50]

Further down the road, scientists are hoping to use gene-splicing techniques to equip crop plants with the ability to manufacture their own nitrogen fertilizers instead of relying on the application of energy-intensive synthetic fertilizers. Leguminous plants such as peas and soybeans obtain nitrogen naturally from bacteria that live in nodules on their roots. These organisms "fix" nitrogen from the atmosphere as part of their normal metabolic processes, and the plant uses the nitrogen compounds in its own growth processes. This process does not occur in cereals and other important food crops, however, and thus a good deal of research is aimed at trying to adapt it to those species.

One line of research seeks to isolate the genes responsible for fixing nitrogen in the root bacteria of leguminous plants and transplant them into the cells of other plants. The result, it is hoped, would be a plant that could synthesize its own nitrogen compounds directly from the atmosphere. There are, however, enormous scientific problems involved in this procedure, and even if it could be accomplished, the result may not be too useful: such genetically engineered plants may have to divert so much of their metabolic energy into making nitrogen fertilizers that there would be little left over to make the desired fruit or grains.

Potentially more promising is research directed toward improving the nitrogen-fixing ability of existing bacteria, a development that should lead to increased yields from leguminous plants. Eventually, it may also be possible to transfer the nitrogen-fixing genes from bacteria associated with legumes to other strains of bacteria known to exist in the roots of cereal crops. If successful, such a development may make fixed nitrogen available to such crops without the plants themselves having to use their own energy in its synthesis.

The chief impact of the new biotechnology techniques so far is to provide scientists with enormously powerful tools for basic research, which are leading to a far deeper understanding of the molecular workings of plants and animals. For example, scientists are only now beginning to understand the complex processes by which plants convert solar energy into plant tissues, and there is as yet only a hazy knowledge of what causes genes to "switch on and off" as they manufacture proteins. As these and other biological processes become better understood, new applications for biotechnology are likely to emerge.

Many of these applications remain highly speculative, but they will not be unmixed blessings even if they do become reality. For one thing, there may be environmental hazards associated with the genetic engineering of bacteria and other microorganisms. The possibility that modified microbes could have unpredictable and perhaps hazardous properties led a group of scientists to call for a suspension of gene-splicing experiments in the early seventies, for example. As Jonathan King, a researcher at Massachusetts Institute of Technology has pointed out, such "biological pollution is qualitatively different from other forms of pollution such as heavy metals, oil, and synthetic chemicals. Organisms reproduce themselves and cannot easily be removed from the ecosystem." Experience during the past few years has diminished such fears, however, and some of the safety precautions that researchers were obliged to follow in government-funded experiments have been relaxed. The fears have not been dismissed entirely, however.[51]

The rapid commercialization of this technology is also creating stresses and strains in some university laboratories, for research that would normally be conducted in the open is now being shrouded in secrecy in case it may be patentable. This change in the usual methods of scientific collaboration is also hampering the traditional free exchange of materials and cell cultures among researchers, according to some reports. Moreover, since many of the small companies that have been started in recent years are based on research findings obtained from publicly funded experiments, there are difficult ethical questions to be raised about the use of knowledge derived from taxpayers' funds for private commercial gain.[52]

Nevertheless, it is clear that recent advances in biological technology are laying the basis for far-reaching changes across a broad range of industries. The way that this technology is developed and applied will clearly have sweeping social and economic consequences.

Technology and Jobs

Although the traditional industries such as automobiles, steel, and chemicals will continue to play leading roles in the world economy in the eighties and beyond, new technologies will undoubtedly have a fundamental impact on employment. Not only are they likely to affect the numbers of jobs available, but they are also likely to influence the types of jobs, the levels of skill required, and the quality of worklife.

Technological change has always played a major role in changing patterns of employment and the organization of work. For example, the technological innovations of the postwar years have been part and parcel of the deep structural changes that have taken place in the industrial labor force. This impact is especially prominent in agriculture, where a combination of technological changes and economic pressures has led to a sharp reduction in the agricultural work force in the developed world. In every major western industrial country, the agricultural labor force now represents less than 10 percent of the working population; in the United States and Britain, the proportion is below 4 percent. However, while the number of agricultural workers has decreased, output has generally risen substantially—a phenomenon that has been dubbed "jobless growth." Now there are indications that in many parts of the world jobless growth is occurring in manufacturing industries as well.[53]

According to studies by the Science Policy Research Unit in Britain, employment in manufacturing industries in most western industrial countries rose steadily in the fifties, began to tail off in the sixties, and declined in the seventies. At the same time, output, while fluctuating in tune with recessions, has increased. "The phenomenon of jobless growth has now become established in the goods producing sectors of the advanced industrial countries caused mainly through technological change," the study suggests. Underlying this trend is the fact that investment in new production technologies has largely sought to rationalize and streamline production processes rather than to expand output at a time of depressed demand and high wage rates. This was especially true of investments in new automobile manufacturing technologies in Britain and the United States during the late seventies.[54]

While these job and investment patterns have been developing, employment in the tertiary sector of the economy—finance, insurance, government, services, and so on—has been expanding rapidly. (See Table 4.1.) In the United States, for example, 92 percent of the new jobs created between 1966 and 1973 were in this sector, and in every major industrial country the tertiary sector now accounts for at least half the labor force.[55] It is important to note that it is increased productivity in the manufacturing industries that has created the economic growth that in turn has led to the increased demand for the services of the tertiary sector.

This employment transition from agriculture to industry, and more recently to the tertiary sector, has not been smooth or even. Some industries have continued to expand their employment, while others, such as steel and textiles, have contracted. Within the service sector, too, growth rates have been highly uneven, with sharp increases in government employment in most countries and steady gains until recently in banking, insurance, and similar occupations.

Technology is not the only factor at work behind these trends. During the seventies, the sharp rises in energy prices, high rates of inflation, and slow rates of productivity growth had deep and very obvious impacts on levels of employment. By the end of the seventies, unemployment stood at more than six million in Europe, about 6 percent of the American work force was out of work, and even in Japan, the official total of unemployed reached one million.[56] These high unemployment totals are in part due to policies designed to dampen demand

Table 4.1. Average Annual Growth in Employment in OECD Countries, 1965–75

Sector	1965–70	1970–75
	(PERCENT)	
Agriculture	−.5	−.5
Industry	.4	−.1
Tertiary	1.2	1.3
Total civilian employment	1.1	.8

Source: Organisation for Economic Cooperation and Development.

in order to bring down rates of inflation. Yet a return to high levels of demand for the products of some labor-intensive industries, such as steel and shipbuilding, is considered unlikely even if inflationary pressures moderate, as the market for these products is reaching saturation.

This gloomy economic environment makes some aspects of technological change at once promising and threatening. The development and application of microelectronics is a case in point. On the one hand, it offers the prospect of enhanced productivity and the chance to revitalize some economic activities. But on the other hand, it threatens to aggravate unemployment in some industries and to reinforce the structural divisions that have been growing in the industrial countries during the past few years as youth unemployment has climbed to epidemic levels and joblessness among blue-collar workers in heavy industries has risen sharply.

Since most of the breakthroughs in microelectronics took place less than a decade ago, it is impossible to draw hard and fast conclusions about the specific impact on job levels as computer-controlled machinery moves into factories and offices and as the much-heralded information society takes shape. It is even more difficult to predict the employment implications of the flowering of biotechnology, because few of its major applications have yet become commercially available. Yet both will have positive and negative job impacts as they alter patterns of economic growth and productivity, and as they change the nature of established industries.

As far as microelectronics is concerned, it is clear that the technology will have a fundamental impact on the types of jobs and the skills needed in the labor force, as some jobs are eliminated through automation and as others are created in new areas. Whether the net change results in greater unemployment depends in large measure on overall rates of economic growth as well as on the speed with which labor-intensive activities, such as the use of solar energy and conservation programs, are developed. Nevertheless, microelectronics can be expected to intensify the trend toward jobless growth in many sectors.

In manufacturing industries, jobs will be created in the production of some electronic goods. For example, the $4 billion now being lavished on electronic watches, calculators, games, and similar novel products has spawned a whole industry that did not even exist a decade ago. But the total number of jobs created in the electronics industry may not be all that large, because as manufacturers incorporate microelectronics into their products in place of mechanical and electromechanical parts, their labor requirements often plummet. For example, an American company, National Cash Register, noted in its 1975 Annual Report that an electronic cash register requires only 25 percent as much labor to produce as its nonelectronic counterpart. As a result, NCR reduced its workforce at plants in the United States and Europe during the late seventies at a time when overall sales expanded. Telecommunications manufacturers in several countries also reported substantial reductions in their workforces as they switched from making electromechanical equipment to electronic products.[57]

A survey of the world electronics industry conducted for the Organisation for Economic Cooperation and Development reported in 1979 that few major electronics companies expected to increase employment over the next few years, even though they anticipated strong sales. The OECD committee noted: "Electronics has dramatic growth prospects ahead in the next decade. If this industry expects to achieve such growth with little or no increase in employment then the question may be asked where in the manufacturing sector is . . . growth in employment to come?"[58]

Many of the industries that have traditionally been leading employers, such as those producing automobiles, chemicals, appliances, and so on, are likely to use microprocessors and computers to automate production lines. Some 200,000 jobs may disappear permanently in the U.S. automobile industry in the eighties as computer-controlled machine tools and robots take over more and more tasks, and a similar number of jobs may be lost in textile manufacturing as automation spreads. Already, newspaper printing jobs have been decimated in many plants as computerized typesetting has radically altered the nature of printing operations, and computerized assembly of television sets in Japan has eliminated thousands of jobs while boosting productivity.[59]

These developments are an extension of trends stretching back for several decades, in which productivity in manufacturing operations is enhanced by the substitution of machinery for people. However, the increased production and incomes made possible by these technological changes have translated into higher demands for goods and services, and the number of jobs has also expanded, especially in the service industries. The key question, therefore, is whether the number of jobs in the tertiary sector will continue to expand to absorb the projected growth in the labor force. There are two chief reasons why the answer could be negative. First, the number of jobs in government offices—an area of substantial employment growth in recent years—may not expand much more because of demands in virtually every country to reduce public expenditure and to cut government payrolls. Second, most observers have predicted that the most far-reaching impacts of microprocessors will be felt in offices and in such service activities as retailing and maintenance work.

The use of computers and other intelligent machines will lead to increased employment in some areas, it should be noted. Computer programming, for example, is a labor-intensive activity that will be a likely source of many thousands of new jobs in the eighties. Demand for programmers is already outstripping supply, and some analysts have even suggested that this shortage could constrain the growth in the use of computers in the coming years. But in most other areas of the tertiary sector, microelectronics is likely to lead to slower rates of employment growth or even to job losses.[60]

In areas such as insurance and banking, which are labor-intensive occupations that rely primarily on printed paper for their transactions, the application of electronic technology could have a major impact. Already, growth in employment in these industries in Europe has begun to tail off, while their business continues to expand. Some observers are suggesting therefore that the jobless growth apparent in agriculture and manufacturing is now occurring in this sector. The most widely publicized of such projections was made in a report to the president of France, which warned that 30 percent of the jobs in the French banking and insurance industries could disappear during the eighties as more and more work is consigned to computers.[61]

The introduction of word processors, computers, and other intelligent business machines will not always cause job losses. In many offices, the machines will be used to improve quality and upgrade services without displacing people. But several studies have suggested that the widespread use of these machines will ultimately lead to job losses in large numbers of offices. For example, a much-quoted, but unpublished, study by Siemens Corporation, a manufacturer of office equipment, has suggested that some 30 percent of office jobs in West Germany could be automated.[62]

Outside the office, microelectronics is likely to affect employment in service occupations ranging from stock handling to mail delivery. The ability to link cash registers to a central computer that monitors stock levels and automatically initiates reordering, for example, will reduce labor requirements in retail operations. As more and more messages are relayed electronically between word processors and computers, a reduction in the amount of paper-based mail can be expected, and hence in the number of people needed to handle it. The increasing use of microelectronic controls in products such as automobiles could change not only the types of maintenance jobs, but also the tools needed to carry them out. A garage lacking highly sophisticated computerized diagnostic equipment, for example, is unlikely to be able to service a computer-controlled automobile.[63]

While it is difficult to determine just how many jobs will be lost or gained by the introduction of microelectronics, Clive Jenkins and Barrie Sherman, officials of a British white-collar trade union, have attempted to draw up estimates for specific industrial groups in Britain. Their overall conclusion is that over the next quarter-century, almost one-fourth of the jobs in the industries they surveyed are likely to disappear. About 5 percent of them would be lost by 1983, they suggest. A more detailed examination of the probable impact of microelectronics on employment in an industrial region in Manchester, England, reached the conclusion that only about 2 percent of the jobs in the area would be lost by 1990 as a direct result of the use of microelectronic technology in both products and processes. The authors of that study, which was conducted at the University of Manchester, warned, however, that "it is in the 1990s that the job losses due to microelectronics will really make themselves felt."[64]

Virtually every expert who has studied the employment impacts of technological change in general and of microelectronics in particular has argued, however, that job losses due to international competition will be much heavier in those countries that do not move swiftly to adopt new production processes and to produce the latest products. The painful example of the Swiss watch industry, which lost 46,000 jobs in the mid-seventies as consumers switched in droves to electronic timepieces made in the United States and Japan, is a case in point. And the American automobile industry, which failed until the late seventies to adopt such energy-saving technologies as front-wheel drive and lighter materials, provides another indication of the consequences of technological backward-ness.[65]

Studies of the impact of technology on jobs have largely been concerned with aggregate gains and losses; few have looked deeply into impacts on the types of jobs affected and on changes in the quality of worklife. Yet these impacts are likely to be just as important as changes in the total number of jobs. A study conducted for the West German government shows just how sweeping the changes are likely to be in the coming years. The spread of microelectronics could lead to the loss of close to two million jobs in that country in the eighties, the study predicted, but if economic growth remains reason-ably strong, a similar number of jobs will be created in occupa-tions associated with computers. The net job impact will not be very great, but the jobs created would require very different skills from those that are lost.[66]

Technological change has always altered the mix of skills needed in the workforce, but the transition to the computer and information society is expected to involve an unprece-dented range of jobs and skills. Already, there are signs of a mismatch in the skill levels available in the workforce and those required by the new technologies, with shortages of computer programmers, people trained in the maintenance of electronic equipment, and similar workers, in the midst of near-record unemployment. Clearly, there will be an immense need for retraining in the years ahead.

In Japan, retraining is largely the responsibility of industry. In some selected industries, employees are given guarantees of lifetime employment, and workers displaced by automation are reassigned to new jobs and taught the skills needed to do them. This system, incidentally, makes the social impacts of techno-logical change in those industries easier for workers to accept since they are guaranteed alternative employment, but it also gives the corporation a far greater degree of control over individual workers than is usual in the West.

In most western countries, retraining is largely left to a mixture of government-sponsored programs and some industrially financed projects. More concerted action by both government and industry is needed. Even *Business Week* has chastised American industry for failing to recognize the importance of sponsoring more retraining efforts. "Managers of U.S. industry have begun to realize that robots will take over an increasing number of assembly lines in the coming decade. But they still think of this as a technological challenge. They have not yet come to grips with the problems of retraining and reemployment it will create," suggested an editorial in the magazine. It added: "U.S. industry cannot leave a retraining program of these dimensions to a public education system that is having trouble teaching simple English and elementary arithmetic."[67]

In addition to changing the numbers and types of jobs in industrial society, technological change can also have a major impact on the way work is organized and controlled. This, in turn, has a central bearing on the quality of worklife. Technology has always played this role. One of the most important features of the Industrial Revolution was the use of technology to organize factory production in place of the old system of "putting out," in which artisans and rural workers supplied textiles, pottery, and other goods to the bankers and merchants, who provided the money and materials. This system of cottage industries involved a scattered workforce that, in David Landes's apt phrase (cited in the first chapter), was not "broken to the inexorable demands of the clock" and which was not easily controlled by the bankers and merchants. "One can understand why the thoughts of employers turned to workshops where the men would be brought together to labor under watchful overseers and to machines that would solve the shortage of manpower while curbing the insolence and dishonesty of the men," Landes writes.[68]

Similarly, the development of mass production and the evolution of the assembly line involved the use of technology to organize and rationalize workers in order to increase efficiency and reduce production costs. One element in this rationalization process is increased control over people on the factory floor as they became consigned to more and more routine tasks that involve little initiative or independent action. The guiding light behind early efforts to organize labor forces in a way that made them unthinking links in a larger process was Frederick Winslow Taylor, an American engineer who coined the term "scientific management." Taylor's ideas, as David Dickson has pointed out, involved breaking down each task into its component parts and then rearranging these tasks in the most "efficient" manner. His thinking, Dickson writes, "launched a fashion for 'industrial' engineering, particularly in the United Kingdom and the U.S., between 1910 and 1930, resulting in techniques that have since become an essential part of industrial processes almost everywhere. In particular, what we now know as 'automation' is conceptually a logical extension of Taylor's scientific management." And the impacts of scientific management were not limited to the capitalist countries of the West. Lenin wrote in 1918 that "we must organize in Russia the study and teaching of the Taylor system and systematically try it out and adopt it to our own ends."[69]

The spreading use of microprocessors and computerized machinery threatens to carry this process even further in some applications, increasing the supervision of workers and further reducing their scope for independent thought and action. In some automobile plants, for example, computers not only control machines, but in many cases, they are also used to control the speed of the production lines and to monitor the output of workers. Harley Shaiken, a former consultant to the United Auto Workers and now a fellow at the Massachusetts Institute of Technology, describes an automobile plant in which a computer-controlled assembly line had been installed: "The system links a large central computer to a microprocessor on a machine. When the machine cycles, it is recorded in [the] central computer. When a machine doesn't produce a part in its allotted time, it is immediately obvious to more than the computer: that information is displayed in the foreman's office and recorded on a computer printout." Under this system, Shaiken states, "the foreman no longer decides to discipline the workers. He merely carries out the 'automatic' decisions of the system."[70]

The telecommunications system has also seen major changes in working conditions in the past few years, as computerized switching systems replace older electromechanical exchanges and as computerized terminals are increasingly employed in the transmission and processing of information. These changes have had a fundamental impact on the jobs of telephone workers who operate and manage the system. Robert Howard, a writer who has studied the impact of these changes on the telecommunications workforce suggests that "the experiences that telephone workers described would have been familiar to the early mechanics and craftsmen in the American automobile industry: traditional skills made obsolete by new technology; jobs fragmented and downgraded to lower pay; work reorganized and rigidly centralized; workers subjected to automatic pacing and monitoring, oversupervision, and job-induced psychological stress. Like the shift from craft to mass production in the auto industry, new technology in telecommunications has eroded workers' sense of control over their work lives."[71]

As computerized machinery becomes more and more common in offices, it is likely to lead to changes in the patterns of clerical work, with jobs broken down into parts and work routed in a way that results in maximum efficiency. It will be possible, moreover, for managers to monitor more closely the output of workers—indeed, an advertisement in the United States for a business computer makes much of the fact that a sales manager can call up an instant analysis showing which members of his sales force are performing above or below average.

There is no immutable reason why technological change should occur in a way that degrades the quality of worklife. But as long as the decisions about the development and introduction of new technology are left solely in the hands of managers, with little or no input from workers, new technologies are likely to increase the hierarchical control of factories and offices. Greater industrial democracy and sharing of decision making are required to ensure that new technologies are not introduced in a way that degrades jobs and de-skills workers. (See Chapter 6.)

The growing international competition among the industrial countries, together with increasing penetration of markets in the rich countries by producers from the Third World, have increased the pressures for technological change. These pressures make it inevitable that new technologies will be developed and applied as swiftly as possible, to push the industrial economies further along the scale of technological advance. The nostalgic hope seems to be that the introduction of new technologies will lead the way back to the golden days of the postwar era, when the world economy expanded at a rate that provided a high demand for goods and services, which in turn created millions of new jobs. Such a development is at best unlikely.

In the fifties and sixties, when there was a felicitous combination of rapid technological change and unprecedented economic growth, the industrial countries were competing for a slice of a rapidly expanding world market. Now they are competing for a slice of a much more constrained market. In short, this means that modernization of domestic industries will be essential to preserve their ability to compete in international markets, but it will not necessarily lead to a major expansion of overall market size. This suggests that Luddite resistance to new technology will ultimately be counterproductive, for failure to adopt new technology courts the risk of massive job losses as domestic industries decline. However, adoption of the new technologies will bring sweeping changes in the organization of work and in the types of skills needed in industrial society. This is the new reality that faces industrial and social policy in the years to come.

5

Technology and Development

The world's economic and technological systems are not working well for either rich or poor countries. The economic problems, mounting energy bills, and rising unemployment levels that have plagued the industrial world in the past decade have affected the developing world even more deeply. For rich and poor countries alike, the upheavals of the seventies have called into question many of the policies and programs that guided economic and technological development during the postwar period.

The global economic dislocations of the past decade have also tightened the web of interdependence between rich and poor countries, bringing to the surface a host of international political, economic, and technological issues. Industrial countries are critically dependent on oil and raw materials from the developing world to fuel their technological systems. Developing countries, as well as many industrial nations, rely on North American wheat and corn for a growing proportion of their food needs. Corporations in the rich countries increasingly count on buyers in the poor countries to boost their sales of technology and manufactured goods. And manufacturers in the developing countries depend on markets in the industrial North to sustain their economic growth.

This growing interdependence means that the economic fortunes of the developing countries are intimately tied to those of the industrial world, and *vice versa.* The problems confronting one region of the world cannot be seen in isolation, for their implications extend around the globe. For example, overconsumption of energy and raw materials by the industrial countries drives up prices for everybody, rich and poor alike. And the growth in the number of people living in absolute poverty in the developing countries not only threatens world peace but it also depresses global economic advancement when the productive capacities of hundreds of millions of people are underemployed.

Virtually all the problems confronting the developing countries, and most of the issues that have surfaced in international economic relations, have critical technological components. As the seventies progressed, it became increasingly clear that fundamental changes were and still are needed in the terms governing the transfer of technologies among countries, in the balance of technological power in the world, and in the types of technology that are generated and applied in different countries.

The Technological World Order

Technological relationships between rich and poor countries rest on two central facts. First, virtually all the development of modern technology takes place in a handful of industrial countries, which possess the bulk of the world's research and development capacity and employ most of its scientists and engineers. Some of this technology is transferred through a variety of channels across national borders, but the imbalance in technological capacity means that the flow between rich and poor countries is almost all one-way. Second, the overwhelming majority of the world's technology is developed and owned by private corporations. Their ownership is protected by legal arrangements such as patents and trademarks and by industrial secrecy, which govern the terms under which technology is transferred around the world.

Throughout much of the postwar period, the global imbalance in technological capacity was not generally regarded as being detrimental to the developing countries. It was widely assumed that the developing countries could bypass some of the costs of generating technology themselves by buying it intact from the industrial world. The central theme in development planning was thus to maximize the flow of technology from rich to poor countries in order to boost industrial and agricultural output. Technology was essentially perceived as a neutral input into economic growth.

Technology is transferred across national borders in many different ways. By far the most prominent disseminators of technology are multinational corporations. They transfer industrial technology by establishing manufacturing plants in foreign countries to produce goods for local markets or for export, they enter into joint ventures with domestic firms that often involve agreements to use patented technology or trademarks under license and sometimes sell the rights to exploit their technologies to unaffiliated foreign enterprises. Multinational corporations do most of their business in the industrial countries, but their investments and licensing arrangements in developing countries are a leading source of technology flow from rich to poor countries—and a leading focus of international debate.[1]

Technology is also transferred in less obvious ways. There has been a vast expansion of the work of international consultants in the past few decades. They advise foreign corporations and governments in their economic planning, and often help determine the choice and suppliers of technology in development projects. Similar roles are played in multinational and bilateral aid agencies, which help to transfer technology by sending scientists and engineers from the industrial countries to work on technology assistance projects in the developing world. And finally, a good deal of technology is transferred indirectly through the education in colleges and universities in the industrial countries of scientists and engineers who then return to their home countries. Many, however, decide to stay on in the industrial countries, as part of the well-known brain drain.

As these technological channels were opened and expanded in the postwar era, the developing countries saw their overall rates of economic growth rise sharply. In the three decades following World War II, their growth performance outstripped that of the industrial countries by a substantial margin, and some sectors of their economies went through fundamental technological changes. But as the seventies progressed, it became apparent that some of the anticipated benefits had not materialized, and new problems arose. The number of people living in absolute poverty increased in spite of the impressive economic expansion. In some of the fastest-growing countries, agricultural output failed to keep pace with rising demand for food, and grain imports rose sharply. Oil-importing developing countries saw their combined oil bills climb from just $2 billion in 1972 to $47 billion in 1980. And as the world economy tightened, developing countries experienced increasing difficulty in expanding their exports to the industrial world.[2]

These problems have prompted a searching inquiry into the assumptions behind the postwar models of economic development, and they have provoked a long-running debate about technological change and the distribution of benefits, both within and among countries. In particular, it has become clear that there are many costs as well as benefits in the transfer of technology from rich to poor countries.[3]

Because of their central role in disseminating commercial technologies around the world, multinational corporations have been the focus of much of this debate. Corporations invest in developing countries and transfer technology across national boundaries for two chief reasons: to make a profit for their shareholders and to gain access to vital materials. As Professor Harry Johnson has pointed out, a multinational corporation "is a competitive profit-seeking institution, not a government with the powers of taxation, and therefore it cannot be expected to assume the responsibility for promoting development in the same way as a development plan undertakes that responsibility." The goals of corporations and the needs of the countries in which they invest may thus not always be consistent.[4]

Multinational corporations can supply the technology, skills, and capital that many governments of developing countries need for their industrialization plans. But the transfer of technology through direct investment, licensing, and other channels often comes at a high price. In particular, many studies have documented instances of overcharging for products and services, restrictions on the use of the transferred technology, and avoidance of taxes through the manipulation of financial flows—not to mention instances of bribery, corruption, and interference in domestic politics, such as the overthrow of the Allende regime in Chile. Less direct costs arise from the technological dependence created by the transfer of sophisticated technology that requires continued imports of spare parts and by the failure to build up the technical skills needed to service imported technologies and to develop a domestic capacity for technological innovation.[5]

These high costs of technology transfer have received exhaustive examination in the past decade from numerous national and international bodies. Throughout much of the seventies, for example, negotiations were conducted at the United Nations Conference on Trade and Development (UNCTAD) to develop a binding code of conduct for the operations of multinational corporations, but little agreement was reached. At the same time, talks aimed at reforming the International Paris Convention governing patents, trademarks, and industrial property dragged on. The developing countries pointed out in these talks that about 90 percent of the patents granted in developing countries were awarded to foreigners and less than 10 percent of these patents were used. This suggests that corporations take out patents in developing countries primarily to preclude others from using their technologies. It is, perhaps, not surprising that these negotiations have made little headway, for they are focused on some of the most complex and difficult issues in international economic relations.[6]

While these talks and studies were taking place, subtle shifts occurred in the balance of power between some developing countries and multinational corporations, as some countries began to build up a capacity for bargaining for better terms for the transfer of technology.

Ronald Muller, a political economist who has long been a critic of the multinationals, argues in his book *Revitalizing America* that "the once-lopsided relationship between the corporations and Third World nations is slowly becoming more balanced as the governments of those nations acquire new wealth, power, and sophistication." Two developments are chiefly responsible for this shift, Muller argues. The first is the fact that American domination in multinational private investment has given way during the past decade to a more competitive environment, as Japanese and European multinationals have stepped up their foreign operations and as some Third World multinationals also have entered the scene. This development has enabled some Third World governments to play the multinationals off against each other to gain increased concessions. China, for example, shopped around extensively for the technology it needed to support its "four modernizations" program, buying from a variety of corporations in the United States, Europe, and Japan.[7]

The second factor that has begun to alter the balance of power between Third World governments and the multinationals is the corporations' "rapacious need for raw materials, labor, and new markets," Muller states. "What was once a David and Goliath contest is being transformed as Third World nations load their slingshots with vital minerals, markets, and new political and economic sophistication." Nowhere is this trend more obvious than in the politics of oil, for most oil-exporting countries have now taken over much of the business of extracting oil and are rapidly developing their own capabilities for refining it as well. These nations have acquired the technology from the oil companies in exchange for agreements that allow the companies continued access to oil supplies.

The growing economic interdependence between rich and poor countries is thus beginning to alter some of the relationships between countries and corporations. The problems have certainly not all been removed, but at least there are signs of progress. Multinational corporate investment is, however, only one aspect of technological development in the Third World. Only a handful of countries are recipients of the bulk of these investments, and even in most of those countries, the investments often benefit only a small fraction of the population.

Needed: One Billion Jobs

Behind the impressive figures on economic growth in the developing countries lurks a variety of disquieting facts. These economic achievements were mostly limited to a few developing countries, and in many of those, the benefits of growth had not trickled down to the poorest people. By the end of the seventies, according to the World Bank, some 800 million people were living in absolute poverty, unable to meet their basic needs for food, shelter, education, and health care.[8]

Economic growth is clearly needed if developing countries are to tackle the immense task of reducing levels of poverty, but growth alone will not be sufficient. One reason why poverty levels have remained high, and why they will be difficult to reduce, can be found in the combination of rapidly swelling labor forces and the rising cost of providing jobs with modern production technologies. A job shortage of colossal proportions has been building up in the developing countries. Until recently it has received little public attention, yet it lies at the heart of much of the poverty in the developing world.

The dimensions of the unemployment problem are notoriously difficult to measure, because few people can afford to be "unemployed," in the western sense of the term, in countries that lack unemployment and welfare services. The poor must support themselves with whatever work they can pick up. That means casual laboring, street peddling, shining shoes, and similar marginal occupations that pay little and are barely productive. Such underemployment represents a vast waste of human resources. According to an estimate by the International Labor Office, nearly 300 million people in the Third World—more than three times the number who have jobs in the United States—were barely eking out a living in marginal occupations in the mid-seventies.[9]

The severity of the underemployment problem differs substantially from country to country. In some, such as the People's Republic of China and Taiwan—countries at opposite ends of the political spectrum—employment of some kind is available for virtually the entire labor force, while on the Indian subcontinent underemployment is already rampant and the labor force is swelling by more than 100,000 people a week. Even in

Brazil, which boasted exceptionally high rates of economic growth during the sixties, at least 30 percent of the labor force was reckoned to be underemployed in the early seventies.[10]

In part a result of population growth during the past few decades, massive underemployment in the developing world has been a long time in the making. It will take even longer to abate. During the first three or four decades of the twentieth century, the developing countries' labor force grew by less than 1 percent a year, but the growth rate has accelerated in the postwar years as unprecedented numbers of young men and women have reached employment age. About 200 million people were added to the Third World's labor force in the seventies, and an additional 700 million are expected to require employment by the turn of the century. Although there have recently been signs that the world's population growth rate has begun to slacken a little, prospects for growth in the labor force in the near future will be affected little because most of those who will be looking for work in the next two decades have already been born.[11]

The developing world thus faces the daunting challenge of finding productive employment for at least 35 million people a year in the next twenty years merely to keep pace with growth in the labor force. Anything less is likely to widen the gulf between those who have productive jobs and those eking out a living on the fringes of the economy. If at the same time productive employment is to be found for those who are already grossly underemployed—a critical dimension of any effort to lift the incomes and the standard of living of the poorest people—about one billion jobs must be found in the developing countries by the year 2000.

Those figures provide the central reason why economic development programs based on modern production technology alone cannot produce adequate social development. The capital-intensive, labor-saving, energy-consuming technologies that predominate in the industrial world make lavish use of the very resources that are scarce and expensive in the developing countries, and at the same time they fail to make the best use of the developing world's most abundant asset—people. Investments in such technology do raise the productivity of a few workers and the gross national product consequently rises. But this approach leaves little capital to aid small farmers, landless laborers, and small-scale manufacturers—producers who now constitute the overwhelming majority of the labor force in most developing countries.

Investments in modern technologies have thus generally failed to provide sufficient jobs to keep pace with growth in labor forces in most Third World countries. As a result, underemployment has risen and urban migration has accelerated as landless laborers and smallholders have left the countryside in a vain search for urban-based industrial jobs. And prospects for the rest of the century are grim if the same strategy is followed. It now costs more than $20,000 in capital investment to establish a single workplace in industry in the United States, and modern industrial jobs are no cheaper to create in the developing world. Thus, to provide one billion jobs through capital-intensive industrial expansion during the next two decades would require a truly staggering level of investment, to say nothing of the energy and raw materials that such a task would require.[12]

But is there any alternative? After all, modern technologies are used in the industrial world because they are spectacularly efficient, and efficiency is an important consideration in developing countries as well. The answer lies in the concept of efficiency. In general, technologies are economically efficient if they blend together the factors of production—land, labor, capital, and raw materials—roughly in proportion to their cost and availability. Since those costs vary from country to country, different countries require different technologies—or at least different mixes of technology—to make the most efficient use of their resources. A country that has a substantial part of its labor force scratching out a bare living in marginal jobs will not make the most efficient use of its resources by encouraging the adoption of production technologies that require large capital expenditures but which employ few people. There can, consequently, be no universal blueprint for an economically appropriate technology.

Such considerations should not lead to the blanket conclusion that all capital-intensive modern technologies are inappropriate in developing countries. Far from it. Often, there may be no feasible alternative. Imported modern technologies may offer significant advantages in the production of goods that are essential for development: China, for example, depended on imported technology for fertilizer production to augment its use of natural fertilizers and its production from small-scale plants long before it began to import other western technologies. And the use of capital-intensive technologies may be justified to speed up processes that lead to increased employment in other sectors of the economy. Access to modern technology on equitable terms is thus an essential requirement for successful development.

Nevertheless, faced with chronic shortages of capital and foreign exchange and with rapidly swelling labor forces, most poor countries need to find ways to raise the productivity of large numbers of people with small expenditures per worker. Economic growth is essential for generating the means to raise standards of living, but the crucial questions are who contributes to economic expansion, and who benefits from it? Or, to use Mahatma Gandhi's apt phrase, is it possible to achieve "production by the masses" rather than mass production by a few?

The question is becoming urgent, for unless economic policies are adjusted to raise the productivity of those who are now on the fringes of the economy—and who have so far been left behind by the technological revolution—there will be little hope of tackling the twin problems of underemployment and poverty. Particularly urgent is the need to generate productive employment in the countryside where most of the people live. Unless that can be achieved, urban migration, which is causing cities to double in size every ten to fifteen years, will condemn hundreds of millions of people to a bleak existence in the slums that now ring most urban centers.

Ensuring that the rural and urban poor share in the fruits of economic growth will require shaping technologies to suit the needs of smallholders, and small-scale manufacturers. But it will also require political and social reforms that will help bring technologies within reach of such producers.

Technology For the Small Producer

In spite of rapid industrial growth in the urban centers of many developing countries during the past few decades, the vast majority of the people remain scattered across the countryside. Some 50 percent of Latin America's population, 80 percent of the people in India and China, and 90 percent of the citizens of some African countries, live in the rural areas. It is in the world's villages, therefore, that productive employment will be most urgently needed in the coming decades; and agriculture, the chief livelihood of the bulk of humanity, will continue to supply most of the jobs.

Yet the bulk of investments in most countries has been channeled into urban-based industries and the rural areas have been relatively neglected, an imbalance that has resulted in a substantial transfer of wealth from the countryside to the cities. Moreover, in the countryside itself, smallholders, who constitute the majority of farmers throughout the third world, have received a disproportionately small share of the rural investments.

There is a pressing need to raise agricultural production in virtually every developing country. Though several successive bumper harvests temporarily removed reports of famine from the headlines in the late seventies, the prospects for the remainder of the century give little reason for excessive optimism. Scores of developing countries are already heavily dependent on food imports to meet their domestic needs, and their food import bills are rising rapidly. In 1980, according to World Bank estimates, the developing world as a whole imported $43 billion worth of food and beverages.[13]

The choice of technology to raise food production can have widespread repercussions on employment and social equity in the rural areas. That lesson has been learned the hard way in recent years. Many countries have encouraged rapid agricultural mechanization by subsidizing imports of tractors and making credit readily available for farmers who want to buy machinery. Such policies seem eminently reasonable, given the spectacular productivity of the American agricultural system, which serves as a model for many developing countries. But the results can be socially catastrophic. Consider, for example, a program designed to bring the benefits of tractors to Pakistani farmers.

In an attempt to raise agricultural production to feed its burgeoning population, the government of Pakistan in the late sixties sought and received a $43 million loan from the World Bank to import 18,000 large tractors. The machines were made available to large landholders on generous credit terms. The technology transfer seemed to work well: farmers who bought tractors increased their output and incomes substantially. But by the early seventies, both the Pakistani government and the World Bank became concerned about the social impact of the program, and the Bank asked economist John McInerney to conduct an investigation. McInerney's findings are revealing, to say the least.[14]

The superior power and speed of the tractors compared with the oxen they replaced enabled each farmer to cultivate a larger area. On the average, McInerney found, the tractorized farms more than doubled in size, a development that forced many smallholders and tenant farmers off their small plots. The use of tractors, moreover, reduced the amount of hired labor employed on the larger farms. Labor requirements per acre dropped by about 40 percent, McInerney found, each tractor resulting in the net loss of about five jobs. The chief aim of the program was to increase agricultural production, but the tractors were found to have virtually no effect on crop yields or on the number of crops grown each year. McInerney concluded that "the distribution of the benefits from the program has been biased in a way that many would regard as socially regressive. If the appropriate accounting procedures were as well defined and widely accepted as financial procedures . . . they would surely show that the widespread introduction of tractors in Pakistan agriculture, if it followed the course that was manifested in the past, would be a little short of a disaster to the economic and social fabric of the rural sector."

On the other hand, that experience does not necessarily indicate that tractors should always be avoided in developing countries. On the contrary, there are many cases in which tractors are the most appropriate technology. The negative social impact of tractors in Pakistan stemmed from the structure of rural society in the country. In common with many countries in Asia and Latin America, landholdings in Pakistan are highly unequal, consisting of a few large spreads and many small farms. Large landholders have traditionally been the first to benefit from technological change because they usually have access to technical expertise and can secure the credit needed to purchase new technologies. Smallholders, on the other hand, are often forced to rely for finance on local moneylenders who charge exorbitant rates of interest. Consequently, irrigation, fertilizers, new seeds, and other yield-increasing technologies usually flow first to the richer farmers, a process that widens the gap between rich and poor. Moreover, the farmers who bought tractors in Pakistan were able to expand their holdings because sharecroppers lacked security of tenure. In short, the introduction of tractors into the country reinforced existing rural inequities.

Similar problems have been encountered with the spread of so-called Green Revolution technologies in many regions. The most widely heralded means of increasing crop yields during the past two decades, the Green Revolution is based on the use of high-yielding varieties of wheat and rice that respond well to large doses of fertilizer. The new seeds can produce at least double the yields of traditional varieties when used under the appropriate conditions. The results have been dramatic. Between 1964 and 1969, thirteen million hectares were planted with high-yielding varieties in Asia, a development that added some sixteen million tons of grain to Asia's food supply—enough to feed ninety million people. India doubled its wheat crop between 1966 and 1972, a feat unmatched by any other large country. More recently, China has greatly expanded its use of high-yielding varieties, purchasing some twenty-three tons of Mexican seeds in the early seventies. By 1977, more than 25 percent of China's wheat fields were sown with Mexican varieties.[15]

But this sweeping agricultural change has brought many problems in its wake. Although high-yielding varieties work as well on small farms as on large holdings, they increase the costs and complexity of production because they require additional use of fertilizers, pesticides, and often irrigation. In countries such as Taiwan and Japan where egalitarian credit systems and technical assistance programs allow small farmers to purchase the necessary inputs and to make the best use of the new seeds, the Green Revolution has not aggravated inequities. But in regions where small producers have difficulty in raising credit and where they lack access to technical assistance, they are less able to take risks with the new technologies. The Green Revolution, like the introduction of tractors, has thus tended to exacerbate existing rural inequities in many settings. Moreover, although the Green Revolution has brought much-needed increases in food production, it has by no means eliminated malnutrition. India, for example, had some twenty million tons of grain in storage in 1978, but millions of Indians were unable to afford sufficient food for an adequate diet. The key to solving malnutrition will thus involve reducing poverty as well as increasing production, a task that will require increased attention to the needs of small farmers and the nurturing of productive, labor-intensive agricultural systems.[16]

That is a far more difficult task than simply raising overall agricultural production by channeling resources to the biggest producers. It will require structural changes in rural society such as the overhaul of credit institutions and land reforms, together with the introduction of technologies suitable for use on small farms and the integration of agriculture with local manufacturing. Many development experts and some governments in Third World countries have recently begun to advocate such a strategy but it requires a strong political commitment to overcome the vested interests that support current rural inequities.[17]

Technologies designed to benefit small farmers and small manufacturers are not necessarily sophisticated. Indeed, in most cases, application of existing knowledge and techniques, such as better use of organic fertilizers, land terracing, more efficient ox-carts, and the application of wind and water power, can raise productivity substantially and lay the basis for further development. What is really needed is the institutional and social structure to ensure that such technologies are available to those who most need them: the vast numbers of people who are now working at pitifully low productivity.

The productivity of small farmers increases sharply when they move from growing a single crop each year to systems of multiple-cropping. Labor economist Harry T. Oshima has found that in Taiwan, for example, there is "no doubt that multiple-cropping, by enabling small farmers to make maximal use of their small acreage and their surplus family labor, contributed to the lowering of the nationwide inequality." But in some rural areas the rhythm of agricultural life may make it difficult for farmers to squeeze more than one crop into a growing season. During planting, weeding, and harvesting, every available person may be busy from dawn to dusk, while at other times of the year jobs are scarce and underemployment is the norm. Thus, if shifting to multiple-cropping requires bringing in the first harvest and preparing the soil in a matter of days, in order to leave sufficient time for the second crop to mature, there may not be enough people available to accomplish the task swiftly enough. Selective mechanization may be required.[18]

Draft oxen, for centuries the chief power source in traditional agriculture, can provide a vast improvement over hand cultivation in small-farm agriculture. A novel project funded by the World Bank, for example, is introducing draft oxen into cotton-growing areas of the Ivory Coast. The aim is to raise the living standards of farm families, whose incomes now amount to less than $100 per year, by enabling them to grow both cotton and food crops on larger plots. It is ironic that the project is encouraging the use in the Ivory Coast of the very technology that the bank was seeking to replace in Pakistan—a change that indicates a marked shift in direction within some parts of the Bank. In another mechanization effort aimed at small farmers, the International Rice Research Institute (IRRI) in the Philippines has developed a range of inexpensive power-tillers that are now being used in several Asian countries.

Irrigation can also dramatically increase productivity, particularly in areas where the climate allows year-round cultivation. But the construction and operation of irrigation systems is often costly and the wealthier farmers are frequently the first to benefit. Cheaper alternatives, suitable for use on small farms, have recently been tested, however. The use of bamboo or baked clay in place of metal filters can cut the cost of a single well point to about $15, and a variety of durable and easily maintained hand and pedal pumps are under development with the support of organizations ranging from appropriate technology groups to the World Bank. Windmills, constructed from local materials and based on a design thousands of years old, have recently been introduced into the Omo Valley in Ethiopia, a development that has helped raise crop yields in a region suffering acute poverty. And the World Bank is also experimenting with a scheme in India that involves renting portable diesel pumps to farmers for short periods, a strategy that spreads the capital cost of the machinery among several users.[19]

Although rural development efforts that concentrate on the needs of small farmers should both raise agricultural production and help reduce inequities, such a strategy alone will be incapable of producing full employment in the rural areas during the coming decades. For one thing, the number of landless laborers has been increasing in many regions during the past few decades, and their employment needs will not necessarily be met by raising the productivity of small farmers. And for another, many small farmers themselves earn part of their income from selling their labor to other people. Off-farm rural jobs will thus be essential in the coming decades. Again, technology can play an important role in generating such jobs, though political changes will also be required.

Rural public works programs, such as the construction of dams, irrigation canals, roads, and buildings, not only provide employment but they also help raise agricultural productivity. Such projects, which consume a large proportion of the rural budgets of many developing countries, are generally of two types. Some employ armies of people to move earth with shovels and headbaskets, while others employ the same technologies in use in the industrial countries—bulldozers, tar spreaders, mechanical diggers, and so on. The former type certainly creates jobs, but it involves heavy toil and takes a long time, while the second type requires large capital expenditure and foreign exchange outlays.

Studies by the International Labour Office and the World Bank have indicated that there is considerable scope for improving the productivity of workers in labor-intensive construction projects by the use of improved wheelbarrows, ox-carts, hand-operated rail carts, block-and-tackle systems, and similar technologies. Use of such technologies, the studies suggest, can raise productivity to the point where labor-intensive construction is often cheaper than the capital-intensive methods. But there is a major drawback: it requires far more organizational skill to manage a vast number of people than it does to operate a few machines.[20]

The Chinese made extensive use of underemployed rural workers in construction programs such as irrigation, terracing, draining waterlogged fields, and constructing roads. Such projects transformed relatively unproductive land into fertile fields, a process that has not only absorbed slack agricultural labor but which has also raised agricultural production, thereby increasing the demand for more agricultural workers.

Manufacturing technologies developed in industrial countries, like agricultural and construction technologies, are often ill-suited to the needs of developing countries. Not only do they require large amounts of capital and provide few jobs, but they also often use materials that are not available locally, produce large volumes of goods for remote markets, and require sophisticated repair and maintenance services. Mounting evidence of such problems has begun to focus attention on the role of small-scale industries in providing employment and promoting development. In many countries, small enterprises, ranging from village artisans to textile producers, constitute the bulk of manufacturing employment. But such enterprises are often shoestring operations, lacking access to capital and established markets.[21]

However, deliberate attempts to foster small-scale industries and integrate them into overall development plans have played a key role in countries as diverse as India, China, Taiwan, Japan, and South Korea. China's rural industries are perhaps the best known. According to one estimate, there may be as many as 500,000 rural industrial units in China, producing a vast range of goods for local needs. It is estimated, for example, that small-scale plants produce half the country's cement, fertilizers, and iron and steel. Since they rely on local materials and produce for local consumers, transportation and distribution costs are kept to a minimum. Like China's rural public works, the rural small-scale industries are geared toward raising agricultural production, a process that creates employment directly in the factories and indirectly in the fields.[22]

Although there has been considerable debate about the efficiency of China's rural industries, a team of American experts who visited the country in 1975 found them to be effective in supporting rural development. The failure of the "backyard" iron and steel plants established during China's Great Leap Forward, suggests, however, that there may be limits to the extent that some technologies can be scaled down and remain economically viable. It also indicates that considerable research and development is required in the establishment of new small-scale enterprises.

Small-scale manufacturing in India has had an uneven history. When Gandhi led the Indian people to independence from Britain, his vision—summed up in the choice of the spinning wheel as the symbol of the independence movement—was of decentralized village production. During the fifties and sixties, however, the Indian government invested heavily in large-scale, urban-based industries and rural industries took a back seat. But rising unemployment in India, coupled with widespread flight from the land, has rekindled interest in decentralized production.[23]

Even during India's heavy industrialization period, some organizations were promoting small-scale manufacturing technologies. Small-scale sugar plants are a case in point. The Planning Action and Research Institute in Uttar Pradesh developed a technology suitable for use in small plants that use locally-grown cane and serve local markets. An investment of 28 million Rupees can establish one large modern plant capable of producing about 12,000 tons of sugar a year with about 900 full-time employees; the same investment can build 47 small plants with an output of 30,000 tons and with a total employment of 10,000 on a part-time basis. The small plants provide village jobs during periods of slack demand for agricultural labor.[24]

Development policies aimed at raising the productivity and the incomes of the poorest people can have important secondary impacts. Their additional incomes are likely to be spent on goods produced by relatively labor-intensive means—agricultural implements, building materials, clothing, bicycles, and so on. Additional income accruing to those who are already relatively wealthy is likely to be spent on imported goods or luxury items produced by capital-intensive technologies—automobiles, television sets, power machinery, and similar items. Similarly, the technologies needed by small farmers and small-scale industries, such as improved plows, bullock carts, hand tools, grain storage bins, brick kilns, and textile machinery, can be produced and repaired locally, while more sophisticated technologies such as tractors and combine harvesters are likely to be imported and require a level of maintenance that is generally only available in the large cities and towns.

Such development efforts may be less spectacular than programs built around shiny new steelmills, massive dams, and modern airports, but they will prove to be just as important.

Meeting Basic Needs

A fundamental change in development thinking occurred in the mid-seventies, as the notion began to take root that the purpose of development is to enhance the well-being of people.

The notion may be obvious, but it represented a radical change from the idea, which had held sway for a generation, that development is synonymous with economic growth. Increasing the incomes and productivity of the poorest people through programs aimed at rural development and the generation of employment is one aspect of a people-centered development effort. Another is the extension of health care, housing, sanitation, water supplies, and other services to those who now lack them.

The so-called basic needs approach to development has not been without its critics. Some Third World spokesmen have argued that the industrial countries' sudden conversion to a new development philosophy is merely a ploy to divert attention from the pressing need to reform international economic relationships. Others have argued that too much emphasis on meeting basic needs will divert resources from productive investments, for increased production is needed to generate the revenues required to tackle the symptoms of underdevelopment. Yet nobody has taken exception to the overall goal of increasing the well-being of the poorest people.

The goal is a formidable one. In 1978, according to World Bank figures, some 550 million people lived in countries where the average life expectancy at birth was less than fifty years, and 400 million people lived in countries where twenty children out of every thousand die between the ages of one and five— twenty times the childhood death rate in the industrial world. Only about one in three people in developing countries has ready access to clean water, and as many as 800 million have no access to even rudimentary health care.[25]

Although decisions concerning the allocation of public funds for services such as health care and housing reflect political choices, the types of technology employed have a strong bearing on the way the benefits are shared. Striking examples of how the choice of technology can determine whether the benefits are available to all sections of the population can be found in health policies.

The most severe health problems of the Third World are malnutrition and infectious and parasitic diseases—illnesses associated with poverty and poor sanitation. Yet the health budgets of many poor countries are heavily weighted toward modern hospitals and sophisticated technologies. This bias, notes a World Bank study, "barely touches health problems in areas beset with serious environmental hazards to health. Furthermore, the resources are typically concentrated on the needs of the urban areas. Rural people are neglected; thus, only a small portion of the total population is granted effective access to modern health care."[26]

There are many explanations for inequitable health care priorities, including past colonial policies that provided curative medicine for expatriate Europeans, medical education systems that are carbon copies of western systems (and which, incidentally, supply many trained doctors to the rich countries as part of a sizable medical brain drain), and hospital services that reflect the demands of the powerful and affluent in developing countries. As Charles Elliott notes, "the results are bizarre. In the Philippines, a country in which much of the population has no health care beyond that of the helot, is to be found one of the most sophisticated cardiology units in the world. In the Ivory Coast, the Centre Hospital Universitaire has facilities that few hospitals in France can rival. . . . Such facilities are used at half capacity, but preempt the lion's share of the recurrent budget of the ministry of health (over 50 percent in both cases)." To those examples might be added the open-heart surgery units in Bogota, the running costs of which are sufficient to provide a pint of milk a day to one-quarter of the city's malnourished children.[27]

Expenditures on expensive medical technologies that soak up the bulk of health budgets in poor countries reflect a choice of providing high-quality medical care to a few rather than meeting the basic health needs of many. In the past few years, however, several developing countries have begun to refocus their health policies, training cadres of paramedical workers and establishing medical facilities in the villages and poor neighborhoods. The World Health Organisation has also adopted a new policy, called primary health care, that also seeks to broaden access to health services and to treat the environmental causes of disease in the Third World. This new policy was the focus of a major conference, sponsored by WHO and the United Nations Children's Fund (UNICEF) in the Soviet Union in 1978, that underscored the point that orthodox western medicine cannot cope with the major health problems confronting the Third World.

A model for many primary health care experiments is China's "barefoot" doctor system, which consists of some 1.6 million people operating in the villages. Trained to use both modern techniques and traditional Chinese medicine, China's barefoot doctors dispense medical care together with advice and training on disease prevention. During the seventies, countries as diverse as Iran, Brazil, Sudan, India, Jamaica, Botswana, Sri Lanka, and Tanzania began to operate such systems. The results can be dramatic. In Sri Lanka, a country with an annual income of less than $200 per person, life expectancy is now approaching that in the United States.[28]

Technologies employed in the provision of health care to people in the villages and poor neighborhoods can range from the simple to the sophisticated. Treatment of diarrhea, for example, has been revolutionized in the past few years by a very simple innovation—giving patients a solution of table salt, sodium bicarbonate, potassium chloride, and glucose to drink. Diarrhea is one of the biggest killers in the Third World. In severe cases, the victim becomes dehydrated and eventually dies from loss of body fluid. The conventional remedy, developed more than a century ago, has been to infuse fluids into the body intravenously. While this may work fine in countries that have adequate hospital facilities for all the population, it is not much use in vast areas of the Third World. Recent tests have shown, however, that giving the correct fluids orally has the same effect. For example, in one trial in a village in India, this treatment, supervised by village health workers, cut the death rate from diarrhea by half.[29]

At the other end of the scale, it may eventually be possible to eradicate such infectious diseases as yellow fever, Rift Valley fever, hemorrhagic fever, and some parasitic diseases by mounting a major research and development program aimed at producing effective vaccines. The eradication of smallpox during the seventies through an extensive vaccination campaign indicates that this approach can be stunningly successful. Yet such magic bullets are few and far between, and they will do little to remove the underlying causes of much disease in the Third World—polluted water supplies, malnutrition, and other effects of poverty. It is worth noting that the incidence of infectious diseases, such as cholera and tuberculosis, declined in the industrial countries well before vaccines were developed against them. Economic development coupled with improved sanitation provided the best cures for these diseases.

The problems of providing adequate sanitation systems in developing countries graphically illustrate the inappropriateness of many western technologies. Cities in Third World countries are growing at an unprecedented pace, outstripping the provision of even the most basic sanitation systems. A World Health Organisation survey conducted in 1975 indicated that the proportion of urban residents connected to sewers in the developing world declined from 27 percent in 1970 to 25 percent in 1975.[30] And even those estimates are widely believed to present an over-optimistic assessment.

It is not simply a lack of resources to develop a sewage system that is hindering progress. A lack of suitable technology is also a problem. The waterborne systems applied throughout the industrial world simply cannot be grafted onto Third World cities and villages where adequate water supplies are unavailable and where suitable treatment and disposal facilities have not been developed. The World Bank, which recently conducted a major study of appropriate technology for sanitation in the developing world, conducted an exhaustive survey of the literature on sewage disposal techniques. Its finding: 96 percent of the research papers published in the field are irrelevant to the needs of the Third World.[31]

Yet there are appropriate techniques available for recycling or disposing of human wastes. Excreta has been used for centuries as a valuable agricultural resource in some countries, where it is collected, composted, and applied to the fields. Even today China's waste disposal system is geared around the collection and composting of human wastes, which are used extensively as fertilizers. Composting, if carried out correctly, kills parasites and bacteria that are involved in human disease. Waterless latrines have also been developed in several countries, and they have been applied successfully in Vietnam, for example.

A survey conducted by Canada's International Development Research Center has pinpointed several different options and strategies for sewage disposal for use in developing countries at both the city and village level. A key finding of the study is that different technologies will be needed in different countries and cultures. "Sewerage has been regarded as a universal solution to waste disposal," the study notes. "The same engineering formulas have been applied, often by the same engineers, whether in Madras, Montreal, Mexico City, or Manila. ... The disadvantage of [this] 'universal' solution [is that it has] so far been able to reach only 6.5 percent of the people in developing countries." The study concluded that the starting point for all sanitation programs should be to understand existing conditions and resources. "Particular options will integrate reuse possibilities that reflect energy, food, or agricultural needs of the particular community. Whether or not such solutions lead ultimately to waterborne sanitation is less important than the fact that they will be the beginning of a dynamic process of development."[32]

The availability of energy is another key element in determining whether people are able to meet their basic needs. The construction of large urban-based electrical generating plants has brought much-needed power to the major cities and industrial centers in the developing countries, but it has also aggravated differences between urban elites and the bulk of the population in the countryside. Professor A. K. N. Reddy has calculated that about 70 percent of the electrical energy consumed in India goes to urban industries, 15 percent goes to other urban consumers, and only about 12 percent is consumed in the villages. Yet about 80 percent of India's people live in the rural areas. Moreover, according to Reddy, electricity is inequitably distributed within the villages themselves: on average, only 15 percent of the households are electrified.[33]

Electricity is, of course, essential for powering heavy industries and its development is an important part of the development process. But if energy systems are founded entirely on large-scale, centralized power plants, social inequities will inevitably increase because few developing countries can afford to extend services to the rural areas. Moreover, the rapid escalation of oil prices and the problems involved in nuclear power suggest that developing countries need to seek alternative energy sources if they are to avoid the mistakes made by the industrial world.

Several studies and recent experiences have indicated that decentralized energy sources—based on direct use of solar energy, small-scale hydroelectric generators, firewood plantations, and biogas plants—can provide energy in Third World villages more cheaply and more equitably than centralized power stations and national grids can. Much of the Third World, moreover, is climatically well-suited to develop and use such renewable energy resources.[34]

Until recently, however, few countries have attempted to build such an energy system. China was a pioneer in some of these developments. Although China's major cities are powered mostly by coal-fired generating plants, the villages derive much of their energy from renewable resources, chiefly biogas, firewood, and small-scale hydroelectric power. According to recent reports, more than seven million biogas units have been built in China, and in 1979, there were reported to be 88,000 rural, small-scale hydroelectric plants in operation. These plants play a key role in powering China's small-scale rural industries.[35]

In many cases, firewood plantations and more efficient wood-burning stoves may offer the best way to meet the energy needs of people in the rural areas. Firewood has been the leading source of fuel for millennia, and it is still the principal form of energy throughout much of the Third World.

But in recent years it has become scarce and expensive as vast regions of the Third World have been stripped of trees by both firewood gatherers and farmers clearing land to produce food. This denudation has caused ecological damage on a vast scale, as the bare hillsides have been exposed to erosion that in turn has reduced the fertility of the land, silted rivers and streams, and caused extensive flooding. It has also caused an energy crisis for hundreds of millions of people who depend on firewood for fuel. Firewood plantations thus serve the dual purpose of providing fuel and preserving the ecosystem. Countries and regions as diverse as China, Gujarat State in India, and South Korea have all begun village-level firewood plantations in the past few years.[36]

But even seemingly "appropriate" technologies can worsen social inequities in some settings. Biogas plants are a case in point. The plants produce methane through the fermentation of a mixture of livestock dung and water (sometimes with the addition of human excrement and crop residues), providing gas for cooking and heating and a pathogen-free slurry that constitutes an excellent fertilizer. The production of these badly needed commodities from waste products seems like a good bargain, but there can be two major drawbacks. First, the plants need manure from at least three cows to produce sufficient gas for a single family, a requirement that restricts their use to relatively wealthy families. And second, in some countries, cattle dung is now collected, dried, and used as a fuel by all villagers; it is essentially a free good. However, the introduction of biogas plants places a premium on dung, which can eliminate the poorest villagers' chief source of fuel. Larger plants serving an entire community may get around this problem, but their introduction would require the establishment of new cooperative arrangements. The point is not that biogas plants are inherently bad—indeed, they are one of the most promising solutions to Third World energy problems in some cases—but that they cannot be introduced thoughtlessly, without new forms of social organization at the village level.[37]

Technologies for housing, water supply, education, and a host of other areas can similarly result in skewed distribution of benefits if they are applied in settings where wide disparities already exist. Developing and using appropriate technologies will not by itself solve problems of social equity, but it will be a key element in social and political changes designed to ensure that the poorest people share in the fruits of development.

Building Technological Capacity

One reason why developing countries have followed in the technological footsteps of the industrial world, instead of developing technologies more suited to their own resources and cultures, is that they generally lack a firmly developed capacity for innovation. This applies not only to the financial and human resources needed to carry out research and development programs but also to the capacity to link research and development to their most pressing needs. It also applies to the capability to control the import of technologies, to choose those that are most suitable, and to adapt imported technology, when necessary, to meet their own requirements.[38]

This lack of capacity is clearly reflected in the distribution of research and development spending among rich and poor countries. With less than 5 percent of the world's expenditures on research and development, the developing world has only a minor influence on the development of modern technology. And even this figure greatly overstates the R&D capacity of most Third World countries, for a handful of the more advanced nations, such as Brazil, India, and Mexico, account for the bulk of the developing world's investment in R&D.[39]

The consequences of this maldistribution of resources are manifold. The most obvious is the fact that the world's R&D capacity is overwhelmingly geared toward meeting the political, economic, and social needs of the rich industrial countries. The $35 billion invested in the advancement of military technology is of little relevance to the needs of the Third World, for example, and even in areas such as health and agriculture, global expenditures are largely aimed at solving problems encountered in the rich, temperate zones.

The World Health Organisation pointed out in 1975 that the spectacular advances in medical knowledge in the past few decades "have as yet hardly begun to be applied to the problems of tropical diseases, where methods of control and treatment have scarcely changed in the past thirty years. It has been estimated that the world's total annual research budget for all tropical infectious diseases is about $30 million per annum; one country alone spends nine times this amount on cancer research. Research in tropical diseases has not yet got off the ground."[40]

The United States Government alone spent about $670 million in 1979 on research and development designed to raise the productivity of American agriculture. This sum far exceeds the agricultural R&D expenditures of all the developing countries put together. And the vast amount of money that has been sunk into developing synthetic fibers completely dwarfs the resources that have been devoted to improving the production and properties of cotton—a crop on which about 125 million of the poorest people of the world depend for their livelihood.[41]

The lack of R&D capacity in Third World countries leads to technological dependence on the industrial world. Not only are new technologies developed outside the economic control of the developing world, but the lack of trained scientists and engineers in developing countries can also put poor countries at a disadvantage in negotiations over the import of technology. As Jan Annerstedt has argued, "Those developing countries that do not even have such a minimal R&D capacity to be able to evaluate different technologies are, in a basic sense, in the hands of those who control the technologies."[42]

Research and development is an expensive activity, and in view of the pressing problems facing most developing countries, investments in R&D often seem irrelevant to national needs. The installation of a thousand irrigation pumps is likely to have a higher priority than the establishment of a plant breeding station, for example. But a few Third World nations have made considerable investments in R&D over the past few years. India's Five-Year Plan calls for the expenditure of about $3 billion on R&D between 1978 and 1983; Mexico spent approximately $360 million in 1978, about 0.6 percent of its GNP; and Brazil spent around $2.5 billion between 1975 and 1978.[43]

Funds for R&D in Third World countries come predominantly from government sources. Of the $484 million spent on R&D in India in 1977, for example, $387 million was provided by the central government, $41 million by state governments, and only $56 million by private industry. One reason for the relatively low share of corporate investment is that the modern industrial sector is usually dominated by subsidiaries of foreign multinational corporations, which perform most of their R&D in centralized laboratories in their home countries. Even when multinationals do carry out research overseas, it tends to be relatively low-level work designed to adapt existing products to local markets.[44]

Third World nations are not the only countries affected by this pattern of expenditure. In Canada, where a substantial portion of the firms are foreign-owned, industrial R&D spending is markedly depressed. Only about 40 percent of Canada's R&D is performed by industry and less than 1 percent of the nation's GNP is devoted to research and development. A Canadian government study recently stated: "One consequence of foreign subsidiaries doing relatively little innovative R&D and being engaged mainly in adapting products to the Canadian market is that they have little to export. Also a heavy dependence on foreign R&D leaves Canadian industry vulnerable to foreign decision-making, both by the parent company and by its government."[45]

This dependence on multinational corporations for technological development can have a stultifying impact on domestic R&D and on the outlook of scientists and engineers in developing countries. J. Leite Lopes, professor of physics at the University Louis Pasteur in France and former president of the Brazilian Physical Society, laments that "if we Latin American scientists and research-engineers hoped one day to be able to contribute to the development of our countries, this hope was shattered by the government decisions taken in the last twenty years to base development on the implantation of foreign affiliates of multinational enterprises." The capacity for technological innovation, he argues, is not transferred by multinational enterprises, and thus technological dependency is perpetuated.[46]

Research and development priorities in developing countries often mirror those in the industrial world, a feature that can make programs marginal to national needs. Rogerio de Cerqueira Leite, professor of physics at the State University of Campinas suggests that in Brazil "scientific and technological research (except in agriculture and health) is rarely related to social and economic needs, and research is often undertaken for reasons of prestige rather than necessity." In India, the Departments of Atomic Energy and Space now account for more than one-third of all government R&D expenditures, more than is spent on agriculture, forestry, and fisheries. And in neighboring Nepal, the government candidly stated in its paper prepared for the August 1979 United Nations Conference on Science and Technology for Development that "the few research institutions that are fairly well equipped with laboratory facilities are mostly engaged in research of their own institutional interests and often of marginal relevance to the broader needs of the country."[47]

Yet there have been some successful efforts in the Third World to develop technologies that have been neglected by the industrial world. Perhaps the best known is Brazil's ambitious program to produce ethanol from sugar cane. Launched in 1975, the program aims to produce sufficient fuel alcohol to meet the nation's automotive needs. By 1980, the program had already achieved the interim goal of providing 20 percent of national gasoline demand. Substantial R&D funds have been invested in the program, and these have resulted in the improvement of established technologies at all stages of the production process. Indeed, Brazil is now regarded as a world leader in the technology.[48]

In Malaysia, a joint government-industry program has helped maintain the market for natural rubber in the face of stiff competition from synthetic materials. The program involved R&D on rubber production and processing. The result, according to B. C. Sekhar, head of the Malaysian Rubber Research and Development Board, is that "the natural rubber industry has not only withstood the competitive pressures exerted by a powerful oligopolistic industry [the synthetic rubber industry] backed by the massive resources of the multinationals and the industrially advanced countries, but has also successfully and substantially carried out a radical face-lifting modernization."[49]

A critical area in which some Third World governments and corporations have begun to invest R&D resources is in the development of renewable energy technologies. Renewable energy resources are likely to play a major role in energy programs designed to benefit the rural poor, and many Third World countries are well placed to take advantage of solar, wind, water, and biomass technologies because of their geographic settings. Scores of public and private programs have been established in developing countries in recent years.

However, because these technologies are also being pursued vigorously by the industrial countries, some observers have warned that multinational corporations may move into Third World markets with technologies transferred from the industrial world and suppress local innovation. Kurt Hoffman of Sussex University has warned, for example, that "we are witnessing within a potentially significant subsector of productive activity . . . the creation of the basic conditions for technological dependence over the long term."[50]

Dependence on industrial-country suppliers of renewable energy technology is different from dependence on imported technology to exploit most other forms of energy, however. The import of nuclear technology, for example, guarantees long-term reliance on imports of nuclear fuel as well as dependence on external technical assistance. Nevertheless, building up the capacity to produce as well as use renewable energy technologies should be a major priority of developing countries in the years ahead.

Simply developing R&D capabilities in developing countries will not ensure that technological development is more in tune with Third World needs and resources, however. In the area of renewable energy, agriculture, and industrial development, there is a danger that R&D efforts will be geared more toward the needs and demands of the elites rather than the basic needs of the bulk of the population. Moreover, all too often, the results of R&D programs do not filter through to the people who are supposed to benefit from them.

The experiences of India and China with two very different approaches to R&D illustrate some of the difficulties of developing programs in the Third World. During the sixties and early seventies, China developed a highly decentralized R&D system in areas such as crop production and health. While a few regional institutes conducted basic and applied research, much of the work in developing and testing new plant varieties and pest control techniques was performed by workers in the communes and production brigades. Many scientists were also sent into the rural areas to work alongside the farmers. The system is widely credited with tailoring new technologies to local needs, but it has also been heavily criticized for neglecting laboratory work. Most of the scientific delegations that visited China in the mid-seventies commented on the poor quality of research facilities, for example.[51]

India, on the other hand, has built up a strong R&D capacity in a range of areas. For example, its scientific institutions are performing advanced work in atomic energy, space research, and heavy engineering, but critics have pointed out that such efforts have not been of much benefit to the rural areas in general and to the rural poor in particular. Both nations are now trying to overcome these drawbacks. In recent years, China has taken bold steps to beef up its research facilities, while India has begun to focus more R&D on the rural areas.

Building up research and development capacity in the Third World is likely to be critical for the long-term economic and political prospects of developing countries. It is not sufficient by itself to guarantee future social and economic progress, however. Most of the problems now facing Third World nations require not research and development but political and social reforms at the national and international level that will allow the poor to benefit from existing technologies. It is always easy for a government to put off making tough political decisions with the excuse that more research and development is needed to explore all the dimensions of a problem. But research and development cannot settle questions of social justice.

Building International Bridges

The growing interdependence of the world economy means that the economic health of the developing world is of vital importance to the prospects facing the industrial countries, just as economic growth in the North is central to the development plans of exporting countries in the South. But this mutuality of interests is not reflected in the efforts of the industrial countries to assist developing countries in building up their technological capacities.

Overall levels of aid from rich to poor countries have not come even remotely close to the United Nations' target of 0.7 percent of the gross national product of the industrial world. Certainly, a handful of countries, such as Sweden and the Netherlands have met the target, but others have fallen well short. And the prospects for the next few years have been dimmed by sluggish economic growth, the election of a conservative administration in the United States that has pledged to cut government spending, and by the policies of the British Government, which essentially has argued that since private capital investments are increasing, official government assistance is not so necessary.

In terms of official support for science and technology, the record is equally poor. There is no shortage of good intentions, enshrined in statements issued from global conferences. For example, the 1979 United Nations Conference on Science and Technology for Development (UNCSTD), pledged to establish a fund for scientific and technological development in the Third World, the intent of which is to build up research and development capacity as well as the capability to ensure that technologies are matched to local needs and resources. But in the year following the conference, the industrial countries generally proved reluctant to make their promised commitments to the fund, and the effort was slow in getting off the ground.[52]

Moreover, in the United States, a proposal to establish a national agency to assist Third World science and technology was torpedoed by the U.S. Congress. To be called the Institute for Scientific and Technological Cooperation, the agency was the centerpiece of the American proposals at UNCSTD. But several U.S. Senators, unimpressed with arguments for the establishment of another aid agency, rejected the idea and voted only a modest increase in the budget of the Agency for International Development to finance scientific and technological programs.[53]

Yet, in spite of these setbacks, there were a few promising developments in the building of technological bridges between North and South. A major attempt to harness science and technology to an attack on Third World food production problems has been launched with the establishment of a network of agricultural research institutes throughout the developing world. The network is funded by private foundations, the Food and Agriculture Organisation, international agencies such as the World Bank, and bilateral aid agencies such as the U.S. Agency for International Development.

The network grew out of the work of the International Wheat and Maize Improvement Center in Mexico and the International Rice Research Institute in the Philippines. Established with support from the Ford and Rockefeller Foundations, these institutes spearheaded the development of the high-yielding varieties of wheat and rice that formed the basis of the so-called Green Revolution. Nine other research institutes have now been established, and their work includes improving livestock production, developing machinery suitable for use on small farms, raising yields of crops such as potatoes and millet, and developing techniques for farming in semiarid areas. The eleven institutes of the network are spread throughout Africa, Asia, and Latin America, and their combined annual budget is close to $100 million.[54]

A similar attempt to mobilize R&D to combat tropical diseases has recently been launched by the World Health Organisation. Like the international agricultural research network, the tropical diseases program will perform most of its work in the developing countries themselves, and local researchers will be trained. And yet another international effort was under discussion in the early eighties for an R&D program on cotton production and the improvement of cotton textiles. The idea is to do for cotton what the Malaysian R&D program has done for natural rubber, and the effort would be jointly financed by the World Bank and the cotton-producing countries themselves. Such efforts have focused considerable resources on critical and long-neglected problems, and there are perhaps other areas, such as the development of small-scale renewable energy technologies, that could benefit from this approach.[55]

If some of the promises inherent in biotechnology become reality in the near future, they could be of immense benefit to the developing world. Moreover, if biotechnology does indeed become a major growth area in the world economy, developing countries need to keep abreast of technological developments. So far, however, almost all the development of biotechnology is taking place in the industrial countries, and much of it has little relevance to the Third World. For example, the production of insulin by genetically modified bacteria is an important and elegant technological feat, but a treatment for diabetes is not one of the most urgent medical needs in developing countries. In recent years, however, some modest efforts have been launched to focus biotechnology R&D on Third World problems and to forge links between researchers in rich and poor countries.

Prominent among these efforts is a multinational program sponsored by the United Nations Educational, Scientific, and

Cultural Organisation, the United Nations Environment Program, and the International Cell Research Organisation. The program supports research and training, conducts surveys of genetic resources, and maintains tissue culture banks. Four centers have been established in developing countries to conduct research and maintain cultures, and two more have been set up in existing institutes in the industrial world. These centers are located in Bangkok, Cairo, Nairobi, and Porto Alegre, and in Brisbane and Stockholm. One central aim of the program is to use the centers to promote regional cooperation on research projects.[56]

Traditional forms of bilateral foreign aid have often been criticized for assisting the rich countries more than the poor. Aid is frequently tied to the purchase of products and equipment from the "donor" country, and it is thus sometimes seen as paving the way for commercial interests to increase their profits from the Third World. Much of the research and development money expended by aid agencies is also directed to researchers in universities in the industrial world instead of being used to build up capacities in the developing countries themselves. But a few agencies established in the past few years are taking a different approach.

Canada's International Development Research Center and the Swedish Agency for Research Cooperation with Developing Countries have both focused their efforts on building up a local capacity for technological innovation in the developing countries. They spend most of their budgets in foreign countries, helping to establish research and development programs, train local researchers, and adapt and apply existing technologies to meet local needs. A similar approach has been attempted by an agency in the United States, called Appropriate Technology International which, after a shaky start, is now supporting projects ranging from the establishment of a small brickmaking plant in Honduras to the development of more efficient cooking stoves in some African countries.

Important though such efforts are, there are few real indications that the industrial world is prepared to put much effort
into building the Third World's technological strength. Partly
for this reason, and partly to become less reliant on assistance
from the industrial countries, several Third World nations, in
conjunction with U.N. agencies, have begun to explore possibilities for technological cooperation among developing countries. Such cooperation is likely to involve the sharing of information on already-developed technologies, the regulation of
technology transfer between nations, and the growth of international engineering consultancy among Third World countries. There are many opportunities for joint R&D efforts as
well.[57]

For example, an important collaborative project undertaken
by the members of the Andean Group of countries—Bolivia,
Columbia, Ecuador, Peru, and Venezuela—has produced a
novel technique for concentrating copper ores. The project,
which grew out of the desire of those countries to manage their
own natural resources, has led to the establishment of a prototype production plant to test the technique. Similar projects
have also been launched by the Andean Group to survey the
forest resources of the region and to develop new technologies
for using tropical forest products.[58]

A slightly different form of technological cooperation among
developing countries was an attempt in early 1979 to extend
China's experience in the development, construction, and
popularization of biogas plants to other countries. The United
Nations Environment Program, together with the Environment Protection Office of China's State Council, conducted a
course in Sichuan Province for officials and engineers from a
score of foreign countries, who were given lectures and site
visits, and participated in the construction of a plant. China,
with its seven million biogas units already in place, leads the
world in this technology.[59]

The scope for a more self-reliant approach to development

through links between developing countries extends well beyond straightforward scientific and technological cooperation. Increasing trade and investment among Third World nations that are at equivalent stages of development at least holds the promise of mutual benefit without some of the problems involved in economic transactions between unequal partners. The problems in forging such links should not be minimized, but the rewards could be immense.

6

Technical Change and Society

Technology has a pervasive impact on society. Less obvious is the influence of society on technology. Technical change and social change have gone hand-in-hand for thousands of years; technological systems underpin economic and social systems, and social and political values and institutions in turn shape both the development and application of technology.

Technological choices, whether in industrial or developing countries, are never made in a political vacuum. The entire innovation process, from basic research to the marketing and use of a new technology, is conditioned by such factors as the profit motive, prestige, national military goals, and social and economic policies. Technical change, in short, is a political process that cannot be separated from the broader forces operating in society. All too often, however, it is viewed as a neutral entity that must simply be "managed" in order to generate net social benefits.

If technological development is to be more compatible with human needs, and more in harmony with the earth's resources, it will be necessary to modify the forces that generate and shape technology. First, although the unfettered workings of the market system are enormously powerful in stimulating the development and application of many technologies, they cannot always be relied upon to steer technological development along socially appropriate paths. Market forces should be relied upon as much as possible, but in many cases they need to be supplemented by government actions. Second, broader public participation in the decisions that lead to the generation and adoption of new technologies is needed to ensure that those most affected by technological change have a role in its planning and to reduce some of its negative social impacts. Third, the immense problems facing developing countries require not only greater access to modern technology on more favorable terms but also the capacity within developing countries to generate and apply technologies more suited to their own needs and resources. And finally, it must be recognized that technology, by itself, cannot solve social and political problems.

Technology and Sustainability

During the past decade, it has become increasingly clear that patterns of production and consumption that are deeply ingrained in industrial and developing countries alike cannot be sustained over the long term. This is most obvious in the consumption of oil and other fossil fuels, but it also applies to the environmental damage caused by intensive resource use, the loss of momentum in world food production while demand for food continues to rise, and the growing disparities between rich and poor. This unsustainability is linked in some cases to the use of technologies developed in an era of cheap and abundant resources.

The link between technology and ecological unsustainability is not new. Some 6,000 years ago, a civilization flourished on the floodplain of the Tigris and Euphrates Rivers (in what is now Iraq), as the development of irrigation technologies turned the desert into fertile land. However, gradually, over the course of several centuries, the fields became a salty wasteland. Crop yields slowly declined, until production was no longer able to sustain the civilization. The problem was caused by waterlogging of the subsoil and by the constant evaporation of irrigation waters, which left behind salty deposits. The soil has not yet recovered, and in parts of southern Iraq, the earth still glistens with encrusted salt. These particular irrigation technologies were not sustainable over the long term.[1]

Unlike civilizations in the past that have been confronted with potentially catastrophic ecological threats and resource limitations, humanity today at least has the ability to predict some dangers in advance. Whether that foresight will lead to corrective action is, however, another matter.

The recent debate in the industrial countries about the need to stimulate innovation in private industry usually boils down to a discussion of how government policies can help foster industrial R&D and remove some of the barriers that hinder the development and use of new technologies. In a tight and increasingly interdependent world economy, this preoccupation with raising levels of innovation and, by extension, productivity, is understandable. Rarely does anybody ask, however, what this surge of innovation would produce, aside from the hoped-for increase in international competitiveness of domestic industries. Indeed, the so-called supply side economics now in vogue, which seeks to stimulate industrial production through tax cuts and similar incentives, has little to say about conservation and efficient use of natural resources. It rests on the assumption that market forces will be sufficient to allocate resources in an effective manner.

Conventional economic theory suggests that changes in the availability of resources result in shifts in relative prices, which in turn cause changes in technology. To some extent, this happens in the real world: oil shortages have resulted in rising prices, and this has stimulated the development of energy conservation technologies and alternative energy systems. But prices do not always reflect the true cost of resources, and the technological system responds slowly to price signals. Moreover, market forces are often swamped by stronger influences on the pattern of technological change.

Among those influences are public policies and the legacy of past technological development. Governments have always strongly influenced trends in technological development, either through direct support for research and development or through subsidies, tax incentives, pricing policies, regulations, and investments in public facilities. Nuclear power, for example, would not have been developed without immense government support; communications satellites owe their existence to a vast infrastructure of hardware and expertise developed through national space programs; and the direction taken by transportation technologies has depended to no small extent on patterns of public expenditure on roads, railroads, docks, and airports. It is no surprise, for example, that the United States, which has seen its railroads deteriorate markedly through lack of public investment, lags behind Japan and Europe in the development of high-speed trains.

Most governments now accept some responsibility for regulating production and consumption to reduce social costs such as pollution, occupational hazards, environmental degradation, and the waste of resources. Although this body of regulation —much of which has been imposed in the past decade—has attracted heavy fire, it is important to note that it has resulted in some welcome shifts in technological innovation and that these shifts are precisely what was intended by the regulations. The development of new technologies to control pollution, improve the efficiency and safety of automobiles, and reduce exposure to hazardous chemicals in the workplace has been spurred by the imposition of regulations in most countries.

Certainly, there is an urgent need for regulatory reform, for most regulations have been imposed piecemeal, some may be too stringent, and many require overly burdensome paperwork. But lost in the current barrage of complaints from business executives and some politicians about the excessive burden of regulation is the important role government policy can play in helping to steer technological resources in more socially and ecologically beneficial directions. A good example is the fuel efficiency standards imposed by the U.S. government in the mid-seventies. These essentially require American car manufacturers to double the average fuel efficiency of new cars between 1975 and 1985, a task that will require unprecedented levels of investment but which will bring the efficiency of American cars close to that of European and Japanese models. In the absence of these standards, the American industry would have moved much more slowly to develop more fuel-efficient products, and it would have been caught in even worse shape when gasoline prices soared in 1979 and consumers turned in droves toward gas-sipping imports.

Regulations can, of course, work against the objective of creating more sustainable patterns of production and consumption—the regulation of oil and gas prices in the United States, for example, has kept the cost of using these resources low and has consequently made investments in energy conservation and alternative energy resources economically less attractive. But regulation is an essential feature of a complex technological society in which the social costs associated with the production and use of goods and services must be balanced against the benefits. Progress toward a sustainable society would certainly not be helped if calls to "get the government off people's backs" were seriously taken to mean a wholesale removal of regulations. Regulation should be used sparingly to enhance market forces and to supplement the workings of the market in areas where it cannot function effectively.

In addition to providing a regulatory environment that helps to steer commercial technologies along more sustainable paths, governments play a direct role in supporting research and development, and they provide many incentives for technological change in some areas. For example, the current pattern of R&D spending, which entails more outlays on military programs than on energy, health, agriculture, and environmental protection combined and which constitutes a huge drain of highly qualified people away from programs more directly linked to economic and social advancement, reflects government priorities. There is a vicious cycle at work here. Part of the reason for the current military buildup is the fear of conflict over control of resources, particularly oil. Yet the continued diversion of R&D funds into military coffers makes it more difficult to pursue technologies that will help to ease dependence on finite resources. In a slowly growing economy, and with increasing restraints on overall government expenditure, increases in military expenditures inevitably result in cutbacks in other areas.

As for direct government subsidies for the development and commercialization of new technologies, billions of dollars are being channeled by governments around the world into programs such as the development of synthetic fuels, nuclear power, and large-scale, centralized generating facilities. By comparison, very little is being spent on incentives to stimulate energy conservation and the use of renewable resources. In the United States, for example, the proposed governmental outlays on the development of synthetic fuels—the production of oil from shale and tar sands and the production of liquid and gaseous fuels from coal—may come to more than $80 billion during the eighties. Yet government spending on mass transit, renewable energy, and energy conservation combined will come to considerably less than this sum, and this is in spite of numerous studies that have concluded that the amount of energy saved by each dollar spent on conservation greatly exceeds the amount that could be gained from each dollar invested in boosting energy supplies. The building of sustainble energy technologies clearly calls for a fundamental overhaul of government priorities and incentives.

In the developing countries, market mechanisms often cannot work to stimulate the development and introduction of technologies that meet the needs of the poor, for the simple reason that the poor are often outside the market system. Unless governments, aid agencies, and community organizations assume direct responsibility for enhancing the technological capacity of small-scale farmers, manufacturers, and others who have been left out of the development process, unsustainable development patterns will persist to the point of total breakdown—as indeed they have in a few areas.

Until recently, it has been assumed that western-style industrial development would be the appropriate model for developing countries to follow. Just as similar technologies are now employed throughout the industrial countries, it was generally anticipated that the world would eventually be transformed into a sort of technological monoculture, with the same agricultural systems, transportation technologies, industrial processes, and building techniques used around the globe. But such assumptions were never valid.

The energy and materials requirements of many modern technologies make their use questionable not only in the developing countries but in the industrial world as well. Moreover, the costs—both in terms of capital requirements and social impacts of massive transfers of technology from rich to poor countries—would be prohibitive. Certainly, many technologies now in use in the industrial world are essential in the developing countries, and international economic reforms together with national policies for the import of technologies are required to ensure that they are transferred on equitable terms. But far from being a technological monoculture, the world of the future will have to be characterized by technological diversity if it is to be socially and ecologically sustainable.

Technology and Democracy

The seventies witnessed a resurgence of interest in participatory democracy. Decentralized decision-making, the right of communities to have some control over their own development, and the need to involve people in the planning and carrying out of development projects all became common buzzwords and even official policy. This trend found expression in local opposition to nuclear power plants, in the formation of community organizations, and in the speeches and sometimes the actions of foreign aid officials. But many of the technological trends of the postwar era ran directly counter to the ideals of participatory democracy.

Decisions affecting the development and use of technologies have become increasingly centralized. As technological systems have become more complex, and as their potential impacts have become more far-reaching, decision making has been delegated more and more to experts, and the control of some technologies has involved constraints on the actions of individuals and communities. This potential conflict between the centralizing influence of technological development and the desire for more control over everyday decisions is the source of much of the ambivalence and even antipathy toward modern technology.

It also lies at the root of much of the attraction of "appropriate" technology. Small-scale energy systems based on renewable resources, such as solar collectors, biogas plants, small hydroelectric and wind generators, and wood stoves, can be developed and controlled by groups or individuals. Organic farming techniques do not bring dependence on faraway manufacturers of fertilizers, herbicides, and other technologies. And the costs of using a bicycle are not dictated by oil companies or oil-producing countries. While such technologies are attractive in their own right in an era of planetary limits, they are doubly attractive in that they offer a way to break some of the dependence on large corporations and government agencies.

But such technologies are not the entire answer to democratic control over technological development. Most people spend half their waking life in workplaces in which they have limited influence over the technologies used and the way they are introduced. Medical care has until recently been synonymous with the use of drugs and sophisticated technologies, prescribed and administered by experts, to treat diseases that could in many cases be prevented by the control of environmental contaminants and better preventive measures; high-technology medical care is of course necessary in many cases, but greater public participation in disease prevention could be both more effective and require less dependence on professional experts. And large-scale technologies ranging from mass transportation to energy supply are often planned, developed, and introduced by central governments with at best token input from the public.

Can public participation be effective in opening up decision making on technological change, so that those affected by it have a greater say in its development? There are no pat answers, for experiments have so far been limited, and in many cases truly democratic participation in technological decisions strikes at the heart of the power structures that have developed in rich and poor countries alike. It is thus not likely to be incorporated smoothly and easily into existing patterns of technological development.

Much of the early discussion about public involvement in technological decision making was centered on the need to educate people about science and technology. "Public Understanding of Science" programs were initiated by government agencies and by scientific organizations in many industrial countries. The rationale behind such ventures is that an informed public is an essential prerequisite for informed decision making. Important though such programs may be, they do not necessarily enhance the people's role in the decision-making processes.

As far as major technological projects are concerned, some governments have begun to take steps to involve members of the public in planning and siting decisions. These include such devices as the publication of environmental impact statements, public inquiries and commissions, the holding of legislative hearings, and in some cases national referenda. Dorothy Nelkin, a professor in Cornell University's Program on Science, Technology, and Society, has studied the efforts of three European governments—Austria, the Netherlands, and Sweden—to involve the public in decisions concerning nuclear policy. She concludes that although "the experiments to date surely represent more an effort to convince the public of the acceptability of government decisions than any real transfer of power," they have resulted in some useful developments. "Even the limited increase in public discussion has influenced government policies," Nelkin argues, and she notes that one result of broadening the decision making in the nuclear area is an increased demand for public participation in other areas.[2]

Public involvement in decision making is severely hampered in many countries by formal and informal restrictions on the release of information about government policies and programs. In a few countries, such as the United States and Sweden, access to public information is guaranteed by law, and even committee meetings are generally open to the public. But in many other countries, government secrecy is the norm, for rigid laws and regulations prohibit the release of information concerning policies and programs when they are in the formative stage. In Britain, for example, the Official Secrets Act prohibits the release of such information as railway timetables before they have been officially announced. In such an environment, public participation in decision making on any matter is severely limited. Public access to public information is a basic democratic right that should be abridged only in special circumstances, such as genuine threats to national security.

Public participation in governmental decisions concerning technology policy does not guarantee that such decisions will be made in the best public interest. But experience so far in the United States suggests that participation, including legal challenges to some programs, has often had beneficial effects. The long battle over the trans-Alaska oil pipeline, for example, led to a project that is likely to cause far less environmental degradation and is publicly much more acceptable than the original proposal. Moreover, it should be noted that environmentalists were among the most vocal supporters of an alternative route for the pipeline, which would bring oil to the fuel-short Midwest instead of having it shipped by tanker to ports on the comparatively oil-rich West Coast. Recently, the oil industry itself has been arguing for a pipeline to transport oil from California to the Midwest.

The intense and at times bitter public debate over the supersonic transport (SST) program in the United States also ultimately resulted in a sound decision not to proceed. Britain and France, which pushed ahead with a joint SST program with little public discussion, found themselves saddled with an aircraft that few airlines want, and which requires so much fuel to operate that it is being run at a loss. British and French taxpayers have subsidized the development and operation of an aircraft that is used primarily by rich businessmen.

While governmental policy for technology is an important arena for public participation, it is in the workplace that most people are most immediately affected by technological change. Public influence over the development and introduction of a new production technology is, however, severely limited.

In general, technological change in factories and offices is governed solely by the decisions of managers. Workers who are affected by the changes are rarely consulted, let alone asked to participate, in the planning of technological change until it is virtually a *fait accompli.* In this context, it is hardly surprising that technological change is often accompanied by resistance and opposition from a workforce that is anxious about the loss of jobs and whose working environment is deeply affected. It is also no surprise that technological change frequently leads to the erosion of skills and increased control over workers.

This is not a new phenomenon. The organization and control of labor has been a feature of technological change since the Industrial Revolution, and the key technological decisions have always been taken by the owners and managers of industry. Recently, however, both managers and workers in some industries have begun to explore possibilities for broadening decision making concerning the development and use of production technologies. These steps have been tentative and there are few firm results, but there are some promising indications.

In the past few years, trade union councils in several European countries have begun to negotiate technology agreements with employers' groups. These can provide useful guidelines for negotiations over the introduction of new technology into local plants.[3]

The first such agreement concerning the introduction of computer technology was signed in May 1975 by the Norwegian Federation of Trade Unions and the Norwegian Employers' Federation, and it was written into law in 1977. The agreement requires full consultation between management and the unions in the planning of new technologies, and it establishes the position of "data steward" in factories where computer technologies are introduced. This is a post filled by a union member responsible for ensuring that complete information on computer systems is made available to workers. In addition, the agreement gives unions access to all data banks maintained by the company. So far, according to preliminary assessments, the law has worked well in reducing the friction generated by technological change and in ensuring that workers have a real input into the design and control of workplace technologies.[4]

As computer technologies become more widespread in factories and offices, such agreements will become more and more important. The British Trade Union Council, partly in response to growing concern over job losses associated with the computerization of work in Britain, has recently put forward a ten-point proposal for negotiations concerning technological change. In addition to the participation of unions in the planning and management of new technologies, the proposal calls for industrial retraining for displaced workers. Greater industrial democracy along these lines will be needed to ensure that the promise of new technologies is not achieved at the expense of degrading jobs and de-skilling workers.[5]

In developing countries, too, the participation of people at all levels in the planning and execution of development programs is usually essential to ensure that technological change is carried out in an effective and equitable manner. Often, when new technologies are introduced with little understanding of the needs, desires, and cultural settings of the people they are supposed to help, they either do not work or they simply reinforce existing disparities in wealth and power. The Third World is littered with machinery that has broken down because people who were expected to use it were not brought into the planning process and they consequently lacked either the skills or the inclination to maintain an alien technology. And the history of development programs is replete with instances of technological change that were intended to aid the poorest people but which benefited chiefly the rich, because the poor had little effective role in the planning and control of the new technology. Participation is not only a democratic principle; it is also an essential requirement for effective and equitable development planning.[6]

In spite of the many problems associated with technological change in the past few decades, science and technology remain the chief hope for overcoming many of the economic and resource constraints that lie ahead in the eighties and beyond. Indeed, in a world beset by oil shortages, sluggish economic growth, rampant inflation, and rising unemployment, technological change has become an imperative. But if the experiences of the postwar years have taught us anything, it is that there are no simple technological fixes for complex social problems. Better weapons and crime detection techniques have not solved the problems of the inner cities, and unprecedented increases in food production have not put food in the mouths of the poor. Moreover, if technological change is brought about through increasingly centralized control and hierarchical organization of society, then technology will aggravate some of society's most pressing problems.

Science and technology are immensely powerful tools that can and must play a critical role in tackling the problems that lie ahead. Public policies that enable science and technology to flourish will be of vital importance in the eighties and beyond. Of equal importance are policies designed to steer technological change along socially beneficial paths and to mitigate the inevitable side-effects of rapid and irreversible change.

Notes

Chapter 1: The God That Limps

1. Stewart Udall, "The Failed American Dream," *Washington Post,* June 12, 1977.
2. Quoted in David Dickson, *The Politics of Alternative Technology* (New York: Universe Books, 1974).
3. Langdon Winner, *Autonomous Technology* (Cambridge, Mass.: M.I.T. Press, 1977).
4. Alvin Toffler, *Future Shock* (New York: Bantam Books, 1971).
5. Emmanuel Mesthene, *Technological Change* (New York: New American Library, 1970).
6. David Landes, *The Unbound Prometheus* (Cambridge, England: Cambridge University Press, 1969).
7. Dickson, *The Politics of Alternative Technology.*
8. David Noble, *America by Design* (New York: Alfred A. Knopf, 1977).
9. There are many different versions of the myths of Hephaestus. For a comprehensive account, see Robert Graves, *The Greek Myths* (New York: Penguin Books, 1955).

Chapter 2: Technology in a New Era

1. Organisation for Economic Cooperation and Development, *Technical Change and Economic Policy* (Paris: 1980).
2. For a good discussion of changes in world oil markets, see Robert Stobaugh and Daniel Yergin, eds., *Energy Future* (New York: Random House, 1979).
3. See, for example, Workshop on Alternative Energy Strategies, *Energy: Global Prospects 1985–2000* (New York: McGraw-Hill Book Company, 1977).
4. U.S. Department of Energy, *Annual Report to the Congress 1979* (Washington, D.C., 1980).
5. For a good discussion of the changing policies of oil-exporting countries, see Walter J. Levy, "Oil and the Decline of the West," *Foreign Affairs,* Summer 1980; Lopez Portillo quote from Alan Riding, "Mexico's Oil Won't Solve All the Problems," *New York Times,* February 4, 1979.
6. Stobaugh, "The End of Easy Oil," in Stobaugh and Yergin, *Energy Future.*
7. U.S. Office of Technology Assessment, *World Petroleum Availability 1980–2000* (Washington, D.C.: October 1980).
8. For a good discussion of the problems involved in developing and executing an energy policy for the United States, see Lester Thurow, *The Zero-Sum Society* (New York: Basic Books, 1980).
9. Lester Brown, Christopher Flavin, and Colin Norman, *Running on Empty* (New York: W.W. Norton & Co., 1979).
10. Demand and Conservation Panel of the Committee on Nuclear and Alternative Energy Systems, "U.S. Energy Demand: Some Low Energy Futures," *Science,* April 14, 1978.
11. For a comprehensive analysis of world food prospects, see Presidential Commission on World Hunger, *Overcoming World Hunger: The Challenge Ahead* (Washington, D.C.: 1980).
12. Lester R. Brown, *The Twenty-Ninth Day: Accommodating Human Needs and Numbers to the Earth's Resources* (New York: W.W. Norton & Co., 1978).
13. U.S. Council on Environmental Quality and Department of State, *The Global 2000 Report to the President* (Washington, D.C.: 1980).
14. Lester R. Brown, *Resources Trends and Population Policy: A Time for Reassessment* (Washington, D.C.: Worldwatch Institute, May 1979).
15. Richard Barnet, *The Lean Years* (New York: Simon and Schuster, 1980); Council on Environmental Quality and Department of State, *Global 2000 Report.*
16. John Walsh, "What to do When the Well Runs Dry," *Science,* November 14, 1980. For a more comprehensive discussion of world water problems, see Robert P. Ambroggi, "Water," *Scientific American,* September 1980; and for an analysis of water problems in rural areas of the Third World, see Robert J. Saunders and Jeremy J. Warford, *Village Water Supply* (Washington, D.C.: World Bank, 1976).
17. Erik Eckholm, *Planting for the Future: Forestry for Human Needs* (Washington, D.C.: Worldwatch Institute, February 1979); Council on Environmental Quality and Department of State, *Global 2000 Report.*
18. Donella H. Meadows *et al., The Limits to Growth* (New York: New American Library, 1972).
19. Robert Fuller, *Inflation: The Rising Cost of Living on a Small Planet* (Washington, D.C.: Worldwatch Institute, January 1980).

20. The Independent Commission on International Development Issues (Brandt Commission), *North-South: A Programme for Survival* (Cambridge, Mass.: M.I.T. Press, 1980). The figures for the Soviet Union are not comparable with those for the noncommunist industrial countries.

21. World Bank, *World Development Report 1980* (Washington, D.C.: 1980).

22. International Labor Office, *Employment, Growth and Basic Needs: A One-World Problem* (New York: Praeger Publishers, for the Overseas Development Council, 1977); Kathleen Newland, *Global Employment and Economic Justice: The Policy Challenge* (Washington, D.C.: Worldwatch Institute, April 1979).

23. For an analysis of these issues, see Frances Stewart, *Technology and Underdevelopment* (Boulder, Co.: Westview Press, 1977).

24. World Bank, *World Development Report 1980*.

25. Estimate of developing countries' oil bill from U.S. Central Intelligence Agency, "Some Perspectives on Oil Availability for the Non-OPEC LDCs," Washington, D.C., September 1980; figures for loans from private banks from World Bank, *World Development Report 1980*.

26. Organisation for Economic Cooperation and Development, *Technical Change and Economic Policy*.

27. Organisation for Economic Cooperation and Development, *Interfutures: Facing the Future; Mastering the Probable and Managing the Unpredictable* (Paris: 1979).

28. U.S. Department of Labor estimates, quoted in Congressional Research Service, "Technology and Trade: Some Indicators of the State of U.S. Industrial Innovation," report prepared for Subcommittee on Trade, Committee on Ways and Means, U.S. House of Representatives, April 21, 1980.

29. U.S. National Science Foundation, *Science Indicators-1978* (Washington, D.C.: 1979).

30. U.N. Commission on Transnational Corporations, *Transnational Corporations in World Development: A Re-Assessment* (New York: 1978).

31. Colin Norman, *Microelectronics at Work: Productivity and Jobs in the World Economy* (Washington, D.C.: Worldwatch Institute, October 1980).

32. Balance of payments figures from U.S. National Science Foundation, *Science Indicators-1978;* Alfred L. Malabre, Jr., "Trade is Playing Fast-Growing Role in Economic Picture of the U.S.," *Wall Street Journal,* November 13, 1980.

33. U.S. National Science Foundation, *Science Indicators-1978.*

34. James Grant, "Soviet Machine Tools: Lagging Technology and Rising Imports," in *Soviet Economy in a Time of Change,* a compendium of papers submitted to the Joint Economic Committee, U.S. Congress, October 1979.

35. See, for example, Kevin Klose, "Soviet Lag in Offshore Oil Technology Has Impact on Prices," *Washington Post,* December 27, 1979.

36. Paul M. Cocks, *Science Policy: USA/USSR, Vol. II* (Washington, D.C.: National Science Foundation, 1980).

37. See, for example, Brandt Commission, *North-South,* and Barbara Ward, "Another Chance for the North?," *Foreign Affairs,* Winter 1980/81.

38. Overseas Development Council, *The United States and World Development, Agenda 1980* (New York: Praeger, for the Overseas Development Council, 1980).

39. Thurow, *The Zero-Sum Society.*

40. U.S. National Science Foundation, "Industrial R&D Rises 11% Between 1976 and 1977," Science Resources Studies Highlights, Washington, D.C., March 9,

1979; Emma Rothschild, "Individual Comment," Annex to Organisation for Economic Cooperation and Development, *Technical Change and Economic Policy.*

Chapter 3: Knowledge and Power

1. Carter quote from David Dickson, "Science Policy in the United States," in Daniel Greenberg, ed., *Science and Government Report International Almanac 1978–79* (Washington, D.C.: Science and Government Report, 1979); Brezhnev quote from Constance Phlipot and Ben Woodbury, "Science Policy in the Soviet Union," in Greenberg, *ibid.*
2. Global expenditure based on extrapolation of data from *UNESCO Statistical Yearbook 1977* (Paris: UNESCO, 1978); Organisation for Economic Cooperation and Development, *International Survey of the Resources Devoted to R&D by OECD Member Countries, International Statistical Year 1975* (Paris: 1979); and other sources.
3. Office of Management and Budget (OMB), *Special Analysis K, Budget of the United States Government, F.Y. 1981* (Washington, D.C.: 1980).
4. The early involvement of industrial corporations with R&D is described in David Noble, *America by Design* (New York: Alfred A. Knopf, 1977).
5. Daniel S. Greenberg, *The Politics of Pure Science* (New York: New American Library, 1967).
6. Willis H. Shapley with Don I. Phillips, *R&D, Industry, and the Economy* (Washington, D.C.: American Association for the Advancement of Science, 1978).
7. Ursula M. Kruse-Vaucienne and John M. Logsdon, *Science and Technology in the Soviet Union: A Profile* (Washington, D.C.: National Science Foundation, 1979).
8. Jan Annerstedt, "A Survey of World Research and Development Efforts," OECD Development Center, Paris, July 1979.
9. U.S. National Science Foundation, *Science Indicators—1978* (Washington, D.C.: 1979).
10. Trends in U.S. expenditures from National Science Foundation, *National Pattern of R&D Resources 1953–1978/9* (Washington, D.C.: 1978), and National Science Foundation, *Federal Funds for Research and Development, Fiscal Years 1978, 1979, and 1980* (Washington, D.C.: 1980).
11. Annerstedt, "A Survey of World Research and Development Efforts"; United Nations Educational, Scientific, and Cultural Organisation, "Estimation of Human and Financial Resources Devoted to R&D at the World and Regional Level," Division of Statistics on Science and Technology, Paris, May 1979.
12. Louvan Nolting and Murray Feshbach, "R&D Employment in the U.S.S.R.," *Science,* February 1, 1980.
13. U.S. figures estimated from OMB, *Special Analysis K;* developing country figures from Annerstedt, "A Survey of World Research and Development Efforts."
14. Extrapolation of trends reported by Ruth Leger Sivard, *World Military and Social Expenditure, 1979* (Leesburg, Va.: WMSE Publications, 1979).
15. Calculated from National Science Foundation, *Science Indicators 1978* and European Economic Commission, *Government Financing of Research and Development 1970–1977* (Luxembourg: 1978).
16. U.S. figures from OMB, *Special Analysis K.*
17. For a critical discussion of the MX program, see Herbert Scoville, *The New York Review,* March 27, 1980.

18. The links between military R&D and the economy are discussed by Emma Roth-schild, "Boom and Bust," *The New York Review*, April 3, 1980; "Research and Government," *The Economist*, July 20, 1978.

19. Simon Ramo, *America's Technology Slip* (New York: John Wiley, 1980).

20. Organisation for Economic Cooperation and Development, *Technical Change and Economic Growth* (Paris: 1980).

21. U.S. figures from OMB, *Special Analysis K*.

22. "The New Military Race in Space," *Business Week*, June 4, 1979.

23. National Academy of Sciences, *Science and Technology: A Five-Year Outlook* (Washington, D.C.: 1979).

24. For a good discussion of the postwar arrangements for science in the United States, see Greenberg, *The Politics of Pure Science*.

25. See National Science Foundation, *National Patterns of Science and Technology Resources 1980* (Washington, D.C.: 1980).

26. Kruse-Vaucienne and Logsdon, *Science and Technology in the Soviet Union*.

27. Derek J. de Solla Price, *Little Science, Big Science* (New York: Columbia University Press, 1963).

28. National Science Foundation, *Science Indicators—1978*.

29. *Ibid.*

30. Quoted in Daniel S. Greenberg, "The Politics of American Science," *New Scientist*, January 17, 1980.

31. U.S. figures from National Science Foundation, *Science Indicators—1976* (Washington, D.C.: 1978); German Research Society findings cited in Organisation for Economic Cooperation and Development, *Science and Technology Policy Outlook* (Paris: 1979); Britain's science expenditures are discussed by David Davies, "Science Policy in Britain," in Daniel S. Greenberg, ed., *Science and Government Report International Almanac 1978–79* (Washington, D.C.: Science and Government Report, 1979).

32. Davies, "Science Policy in Britain."

33. Bruce L. R. Smith and Joseph J. Karlesky, *The State of Academic Science* (New Rochelle, N.Y.: Change Magazine Press, 1977).

34. John D. Holmfeld, "Dilemmas Down the Road," *The Wilson Quarterly*, Summer 1978.

35. American Association for the Advancement of Science (AAAS), *Intersociety Preliminary Analysis of R&D in the F.Y. 1980 Budget* (Washington, D.C.: 1979).

36. International Energy Agency, *Energy Policies and Programs of IEA Countries 1977* (Paris: 1979).

37. International Energy Agency, *Energy Policies and Programs of IEA Countries 1979* (Paris: 1980); AAAS, *R&D in the F.Y. 1980 Budget*.

38. International Energy Agency, *Energy Policies 1979*.

39. *Ibid.*

40. Figures for government share of industrial R&D funding from OECD, *International Statistical Year 1975*.

41. U.S. aerospace, telecommunications, and electrical equipment expenditures from National Science Foundation, "Industrial R&D Rises 11% Between 1976 and 1977," Science Resources Studies Highlights, Washington, D.C., March 9, 1979; French data from Government of France, *Enveloppe Recherche en 1979* (Paris: 1979).

42. "Scorecard for Corporate R&D Expenditures," *Business Week*, July 7, 1980.

43. Organisation for Economic Cooperation and Development, *Trends in Industrial R&D* (Paris: 1979).

44. Organisation for Economic Cooperation and Development, *Technical Change and Economic Policy.*

45. National Science Foundation, *Science Indicators—1976.*

46. Organisation for Economic Cooperation and Development, *Trends in Industrial R&D.*

47. Richard Nelson, "Technical Advance and Economic Growth," paper prepared for International Conference on Science and Technology, New York University, March 1979; see also Organisation for Economic Cooperation and Development, *Technical Change and Economic Policy* (Paris: 1980).

Chapter 4: Innovation, Productivity, and Jobs

1. For a more complete discussion of the impact of microelectronics, see Colin Norman, *Microelectronics at Work: Productivity and Jobs in the World Economy* (Washington, D.C.: Worldwatch Institute, October 1980).

2. Ronald Muller, *Revitalizing America* (New York: Simon and Schuster, 1980).

3. Michael Harrington, "The Productivity Ploy," *New York Times*, March 21, 1980.

4. Edward F. Denison, *Accounting for Slower Economic Growth* (Washington, D.C.: Brookings Institution, 1979).

5. Congressional Research Service, "Technology and Trade: Some Indicators of the State of U.S. Industrial Innovation," report prepared for Subcommittee on Trade, Committee on Ways and Means, U.S. House of Representatives, April 21, 1980.

6. Tim Metz, "New Issues Become the Rage Again, Riding on Stock Market's Strength," *Wall Street Journal*, November 17, 1980.

7. "High Technology, Wave of the Future or a Market Flash in the Pan?," *Business Week*, November 10, 1980; Carl Burgen, "The Bulls are Back in Venture Capital," *New York Times*, August 17, 1980.

8. Office of Technology Assessment, *Technology and Steel Industry Competitiveness* (Washington, D.C.: U.S. Congress, 1980). It should be noted, however, that lack of capital is not the only reason that steel companies have not upgraded their plants. Instead of investing in new equipment, some leading U.S. companies have used capital to take over non-steel corporations in the past few years.

9. Organisation for Economic Cooperation and Development, *Technical Change and Economic Policy* (Paris: 1980).

10. "Chemicals: A Survey," *The Economist*, April 7, 1979.

11. Lester R. Brown, *The Worldwide Loss of Cropland* (Washington, D.C.: Worldwatch Institute, October 1978).

12. *Ibid.*

13. For an examination of technological trends in the fertilizer and pesticides industries, see Bruna Teso, *Sector Report: The Fertilizers and Pesticides Industry*, background study prepared for Organisation for Economic Cooperation and Development, *Technical Change and Economic Policy.*

14. L. M. Thompson, "Weather, Variability, Climatic Change, and Grain Production," *Science*, May 9, 1975; Neal Jensen, "Limits to Growth in World Food Production," *Science*, July 28, 1978.

15. Jay W. Forrester, "Changing Economic Patterns," *Technology Review*, August/September 1978.

16. National Academy of Sciences, *Microstructure Science, Engineering, and Technology* (Washington, D.C.: 1979).

17. A general description and history of computers and microelectronics is given in Christopher Evans, *The Micro Millennium* (New York: Viking Press, 1980); more detailed descriptions of microelectronic technologies are contained in several articles in the September 1977 issue of *Scientific American* and in an excellent series of articles by Arthur L. Robinson in the issues of *Science* of May 2, May 9, and May 30, June 13, and July 11, 1980.

18. Arthur L. Robinson, "Perilous Times for U.S. Microcircuit Makers," *Science*, May 9, 1980.

19. The impact of demand for military and space programs on the development of microelectronics is discussed in Charles River Associates, *Innovation, Competition, and Government Policy in the Semiconductor Industry* (Boston: 1980).

20. Estimates of sales and growth rates are derived from figures in Semiconductor Industry Association, *1979 Yearbook and Directory* (Cupertino, Calif.: 1980); Charles River Associates, *Innovation, Competition, and Government Policy;* and Electronic Industries Association, *Electronic Market Data Book 1980* (Washington, D.C.: 1980).

21. Estimate of sales of electronic consumer goods is from "Microelectronics Survey," *The Economist*, March 1, 1980. It consists of $1 billion for toys and games, $1.5 billion for calculators, and $1.7 billion for watches.

22. The use of computers in continuous-process industries is described by Stephen Kahne, Irving Lefkowitz, and Charles Rose, "Automatic Control by Distributed Intelligence," *Scientific American*, June 1979.

23. See, for example, Peter Marsh, "Towards the Unmanned Factory," *New Scientist*, July 31, 1980, and European Trade Union Institute (ETUI), *The Impact of Microelectronics on Employment in Western Europe in the 1980's* (Brussels: 1979). This study is an excellent source of information on the uses and impacts of microprocessors.

24. Zama plant figures from "The Longbridge Robots Will March over the Transport Union," *The Economist*, April 19, 1980; Estes prediction quoted by Harley Shaiken, "Detroit Downsizes U.S. Jobs," *The Nation*, October 11, 1980.

25. Peter Marsh, "Robots See the Light," *New Scientist*, June 12, 1980.

26. "Robots Join the Labor Force," *Business Week*, June 9, 1980.

27. Marsh, "Robots See the Light"; Engelberger estimate quoted in Peter Marsh, "Britain Grapples with Robots," *New Scientist*, April 24, 1980; sales projections quoted in "Robots Join the Labor Force," *Business Week*.

28. ETUI, *Impact of Microelectronics on Employment.*

29. "Robots Join the Labor Force," *Business Week.*

30. Jon Stewart, "The Inhuman Office of the Future," *Saturday Review*, June 23, 1979.

31. Electronic Industries Association, *Electronic Market Data Book 1980.*

32. ETUI, *Impact of Microelectronics on Employment.* For a discussion of these potential developments, see Evans, *The Micro Millennium,* and Iann Barron and Ray Curnow, *The Future with Microelectronics* (London: Frances Pinter, Ltd., 1979).

33. Working Women, "Race Against Time: Automation of the Office," Cleveland, Ohio, April 1980.

34. Organisation for Economic Cooperation and Development, *Interfutures: Facing the Future; Mastering the Probable and Managing the Unpredictable* (Paris: 1979).

35. U.K. Government, "Microelectronics: Challenge and Response," Memorandum by the Secretaries of State for Industry, Employment, and Education and Science, London, November 1978; Simon Nora and Alain Minc, *The Computerization of Society* (Cambridge, Mass.: MIT Press, 1980). This report was originally published by the French Government as *L'Informatisation de la Société* (Paris: La Documentation Française, 1978).

36. Charles River Associates, *Innovation, Competition, and Government Policy.*

37. For a discussion of Japan's programs, see Gene Gregory, "The March of the Japanese Micro," *New Scientist*, October 11, 1979. See also Robinson, "Perilous Times for U.S. Microcircuit Makers," Charles River Associates, *Innovation, Competition, and Government Policy,"* and "Japan Stuns the Americans," *The Economist*, February 23, 1980.

38. Bro Uttal, "Europe's Wild Swing at the Silicon Giants," *Fortune*, July 28, 1980; Guy de Jonquieres, "Why Inmos Got Its £25 Million," *Financial Times*, July 31, 1980.

39. Organisation for Economic Cooperation and Development, *Interfutures.*

40. Uttal, "Europe's Wild Swing."

41. Tim Metz, "New Genentech Issue Trades Wildly as Investors Seek Latest High-Flier," *Wall Street Journal*, October 15, 1980.

42. Commission of the European Communities, "Tomorrow's Bio-Society," European File, July 1980. For a more comprehensive discussion of the potential for biotechnology, see Congressional Research Service, "Genetic Engineering, Human Genetics, and Cell Biology," report prepared for the Subcommittee on Science, Research, and Technology, Committee on Science and Technology, U.S. House of Representatives, August 1980.

43. See, for example, "DuPont: Seeking a Future in Biosciences," *Business Week*, November 24, 1980.

44. Nicholas Wade, "Hot Genes," *New Republic*, November 8, 1980.

45. Estimates for interferon sales from "Challenging the U.S. Lead in Biotechnology," *Business Week*, August 4, 1980.

46. "Get Set for Biotechnology," *Chemical Week*, October 8, 1980.

47. Jerry Bishop, "National Distillers Plans Major Project to Turn Corn to Alcohol in Secret Process," *Wall Street Journal*, October 24, 1980.

48. "Where Genetic Engineering Will Change Industry," *Business Week*, October 22, 1979.

49. "The Second Green Revolution," *Business Week*, August 26, 1980.

50. W. Hugh Bollinger, "Sustaining Renewable Resources: Techniques from Applied Botany," in *Techniques from Applied Botany* (New York: Academic Press, 1980); Unilever palm oil project report by Steve Galante, "Unilever Researchers Try Cloning a Bid to Increase Malaysian Palm Oil Output," *Wall Street Journal*, June 30, 1980.

51. Jonathan King, "New Genetic Technologies: Prospects and Hazards," *Technology Review*, February 1980.

52. See, for example, Nicholas Wade, "Hot Genes," and Hal Lancaster, "Profits in Gene Splicing Bring Tangled Issue of Ownership to Fore," *Wall Street Journal*, December 3, 1980.

53. Roy Rothwell and Walter Zegveld, *Technical Change and Employment* (New York: St. Martin's Press, 1979).

54. *Ibid.*

55. Organisation for Economic Cooperation and Development, *A Medium Term Strategy for Employment and Manpower Policies* (Paris: 1978).

56. Kathleen Newland, *Global Employment and Economic Justice: The Policy Challenge* (Washington, D.C.: Worldwatch Institute, April 1979).

57. ETUI, *Impact of Microelectronics on Employment*, and Colin Hines and Graham Searle, *Automatic Unemployment* (London: Earth Resources Research, 1979).

58. Mick McLean, *Sector Report: The Electronics Industry*, background study prepared for Organisation for Economic Cooperation and Development, *Technical Change and Economic Policy*.

59. Automobile industry estimates from Harley Shaiken, "Detroit Downsizes Jobs." For general estimates of job losses see, for example, Clive Jenkins and Barrie Sherman, *The Collapse of Work* (London: Eyre Methuen, 1979).

60. See, for example, "Missing Computer Software," *Business Week*, September 1, 1980.

61. European Economic Commission, *Population and Employment* (Brussels: 1979); Nora and Minc, *The Computerization of Society*.

62. David Dangelmayer, "The Job Killers of Germany," *New Scientist*, June 8, 1978.

63. See, for example, Barron and Curnow, *The Future With Microelectronics*.

64. Jenkins and Sherman, *Collapse of Work;* Rod Coombs and Ken Green, "Slow March of the Microchip," *New Scientist*, August 7, 1980.

65. Swiss figures from ETUI, *Impact of Microelectronics on Employment.*

66. Findings cited by Robert Walgate, "German Workforce: Ten Years On," *Nature*, August 28, 1980.

67. "When the Robots Move In," *Business Week*, June 9, 1980.

68. David Landes, *The Unbound Prometheus* (Cambridge, England: Cambridge University Press, 1969).

69. David Dickson, *The Politics of Alternative Technology* (New York: Universe Books, 1974).

70. Harley Shaiken, "The Brave New World of Work in Auto," *In These Times*, September 19–25, 1979.

71. Robert Howard, "Brave New Workplace," *Working Papers*, November/December 1980.

Chapter 5: Technology and Development

1. The literature on technology transfer is voluminous. For a cross-section of views, see the collection of papers published in Jairam Ramesh and Charles Weiss, Jr., eds., *Mobilizing Technology for World Development* (New York: Praeger Publishers, 1979). For a discussion of the conflicts involved in technology transfer, see Denis Goulet, *The Uncertain Promise* (New York: IDOC/North America 1977), and Frances Stewart, *Technology and Underdevelopment* (Boulder, Co.: Westview Press, 1977).

2. For a description of the growth rates achieved in the postwar period, see David Morawetz, *Twenty-Five Years of Economic Development 1950 to 1975* (Washington, D.C.: World Bank, 1977). Figures for oil import bills from U.S. Central Intelligence Agency, "Some Perspectives on Oil Availability for the Non-OPEC LDCs," Washington, D.C., September 1980.

3. For a discussion of the changing prospects facing developing countries, see World Bank, *World Development Report 1980* (Washington, D.C.: 1980), John Sewell and the staff of the Overseas Development Council, *The United States and World Development, Agenda 1980* (New York: Praeger Publishers, 1980), and Independent Commission on International Development Issues (Brandt Commission), *North-South* (Cambridge, Mass.: MIT Press, 1980).

4. Harry A. Johnson, *Technology and Economic Interdependence* (New York: St. Martin's Press, 1975).

5. For a discussion of these costs, see, for example, Goulet, *The Uncertain Promise;* Frances Stewart, "International Transfer: Issues and Policy Options," World Bank Staff Working Paper No. 344, Washington, D.C., July 1979; and United Nations Conference on Trade and Development, "Transfer of Technology: Its Implications for Development and Environment," New York, 1978.

6. See G. K. Helleiner, "International Technology Issues: Southern Needs and Northern Responses," in Ramesh and Weiss, eds., *Mobilizing Technology.*

7. Ronald Muller, *Revitalizing America* (New York: Simon and Schuster, 1980).

8. World Bank, *World Development Report 1980.*

9. International Labour Office, *Employment, Growth, and Basic Needs: A One-World Problem* (New York: Praeger Publishers, for the Overseas Development Council, 1977).

10. For an analysis of employment in China, see Thomas Rawski, "Industrialization, Technology, and Employment in the People's Republic of China," World Bank Staff Working Paper No. 291, Washington, D.C., August 1978; Brazil's employment prospects are discussed in World Bank, *Brazil, Human Resources Special Report* (Washington, D.C.: 1979).

11. International Labour Office, "World and Regional Labour Force Prospects to the Year 2000," in *The Population Debate: Dimensions and Perspectives, Papers of the World Population Conference* (New York: United Nations, 1975).

12. There are few good estimates of the capital costs of providing jobs in industry, but the costs do not differ much in modern industries established in developing or industrial countries. The Conference Board has estimated that the capital investment per job in the United States ranges from $108,000 per employee in the petrochemicals industry to $5,000 in the clothing industry, with an average of about $20,000 in all industries. See Richard Grossman and Gail Daneker, *Jobs and Energy* (Washington, D.C.: Environmentalists for Full Employment, 1977).

13. World Bank, *World Development Report 1980.*

14. John P. McInerney *et al.*, "The Consequences of Farm Tractors in Pakistan," World Bank, Washington, D.C., 1975.

15. Lester R. Brown, *The Twenty-Ninth Day: Accommodating Human Needs and Numbers to the Earth's Resources* (New York: W. W. Norton & Co., 1978); Chinese figures from Dana Dalrymple, "Development and Spread of High-Yielding Varieties of Wheat and Rice in the Less Developed Nations," U.S. Department of Agriculture, Washington, D.C., September 1978.

16. The Green Revolution has been exhaustively examined. For a critical account, see Keith Griffin, *The Green Revolution: An Economic Analysis* (Geneva: United Nations Institute for Social Development, 1972), and for a later, more detailed analysis, see B. H. Farmer, ed., *Green Revolution?* (London: Macmillan, 1978).

17. See, for example, Hans Singer, *Technologies for Basic Needs* (Geneva: International Labour Office, 1977) and Frances Stewart, *Technology and Underdevelopment.*

18. Harry T. Oshima, "Multiple-cropping in Asian Development: Summary and Further Research," *The Philippine Economic Journal,* Vol. 14, Nos. 1 and 2, 1975.

19. World Bank, "Appropriate Technology in World Bank Activities," Washington, D.C., July 1976; Denis N. Fernando, "Low-Cost Tube Wells," *Appropriate Tech-*

nology, Vol. 2, No. 4, 1976; World Bank, "Appropriate Technology"; Peter Fraenkel, "Food from Wind in Ethiopia," *Appropriate Technology*, Vol. 2, No. 4, 1976.

20. World Bank, *Appropriate Technology and World Bank Assistance to the Poor*, S & T Report No. 29, Washington, D.C., December 1977; M. Allal *et al.*, "Development and Promotion of Appropriate Road Construction Technology," *International Labour Review*, September/October 1977.

21. For an excellent discussion of the informal sector's role in development, see Paul Harrison, *Inside the Third World* (London: Penguin, 1979).

22. American Rural Small-Scale Industry Delegation, *Rural Small-Scale Industry in the People's Republic of China* (Berkeley: University of California Press, 1977).

23. India's industrial development is analyzed in John W. Mellor, *The New Economics of Growth* (Ithaca, N.Y.: Cornell University, 1976).

24. M. K. Garg, "The Scaling-Down of Modern Technology: Crystal Sugar Manufacturing in India," in Nicholas Jequier, ed., *Appropriate Technology: Problems and Promises* (Paris: Organisation for Economic Cooperation and Development, 1976).

25. World Bank, *World Development Report 1980*.

26. *Ibid.*

27. Charles Elliott, *Patterns of Poverty in the Third World* (New York: Praeger Publishers, 1975); Richard Jolly, "International Dimensions," in Hollis Chenery, ed., *Redistribution With Growth* (London: Oxford University Press, 1974).

28. World Bank, *World Development Report 1980*.

29. Anil Agarwal, "A Cure for a Killer—But How to Deliver It?" *Nature*, March 29, 1979.

30. World Health Organization figures cited in Witold Rybczynski, *et al.*, *Low-Cost Technology Options for Sanitation* (Ottawa: International Development Research Center, 1978).

31. World Bank, "Appropriate Technology for Water Supply and Waste Disposal," Progress Report, Washington, D.C., June 1977.

32. Rybczynski *et al.*, *Low-Cost Options*.

33. C. R. Prasad, K. Krishna Prasad, and A. K. N. Reddy, "Biogas Plants: Prospects, Problems and Tasks," *Economic and Political Weekly*, August 1974.

34. See, for example, Denis Hayes, *Energy for Development: Third World Options* (Washington, D.C.: Worldwatch Institute, December 1977).

35. Figures for biogas plants from Qu Geping, "China Turns to Biogas," *Mazingira*, Vol. 12, 1980; small-scale hydroelectric figures from Central Intelligence Agency, "Electric Power for China's Modernization: The Hydroelectric Option," Washington, D.C., May 1980.

36. Erik Eckholm, *Planting for the Future: Forestry for Human Needs* (Washington, D.C.: Worldwatch Institute, February 1979).

37. Prasad *et al.*, "Biogas Plants."

38. See, for example, Stewart, "International Technology Transfer."

39. Jan Annerstedt, "A Survey of World Research and Development Efforts," OECD Development Center, Paris, July 1979.

40. World Health Organization, *Tropical Diseases—The Challenge and the Opportunity* (Geneva: 1975).

41. U.S. agricultural R&D figures from U.S. National Science Foundation (NSF), *Federal Funds for Research and Development, Fiscal Years 1978, 1979, and 1980* (Washington, D.C.: 1980).

42. Annerstedt, "A Survey of World R&D."
43. M. Anandakrishnan, "Science Policy in India," in Daniel Greenberg, ed., *Science and Government Report International Almanac 1978–79* (Washington, D.C.: Science and Government Report, 1979); Edmundo Flores, "Mexico's Program for Science and Technology, 1978 to 1982," *Science,* June 22, 1979; Rogerio de Cerqueira Leite, "Science Policy in Brazil," in Greenberg, *Science and Government Almanac.*
44. Anandakrishnan, "Science Policy in India"; discussion of type of overseas R&D performed by U.S. multinational corporations from NSF, "U.S. Industrial R&D Spending Abroad," *Reviews of Data on Science Resources,* NSF, April 1979.
45. Quote from David Spurgeon, "Science Policy in Canada," in Greenberg, *Science and Government Almanac.*
46. J. Leite Lopes, "Science and the Making of Society in Latin America," *Interciencia,* May/June 1980.
47. Leite, "Science Policy in Brazil"; Anandakrishnan, "Science Policy in India"; Nepalese quote from Jan Annerstedt, "Indigenous R&D Capacities and International Diplomacy," Roskilde University, Denmark, 1979.
48. For a review of Brazil's alcohol program, see Trevor Lones, "Brazil Avoids Hiccups With Alcoholic Car Fuels," *New Scientist,* April 18, 1980.
49. B. H. Sekhar, "Malaysian Rubber in the World Market," in Ramesh and Weiss, *Mobilizing Technology.*
50. Kurt Hoffmann, "Alternative Energy Technologies and Third World Rural Energy Needs: A Case of Emerging Technological Dependency," *Development and Change,* Vol. 2, 1980.
51. For a review of China's science policy, see Boel Berner, "The Organization and Planning of Scientific Research in China Today," Discussion Paper No. 134, Research Policy Unit, University of Lund, November 1979.
52. David Dickson, "Congress Turns Sour on Technology Fund," *Nature,* August 7, 1980; Stephanie Yanchinski, "The West Undermines UNCSTD," *New Scientist,* December 13, 1979.
53. "Big Promises, Little Cash for 3rd World R&D," *Science and Government and Report,* September 1, 1980.
54. Consultative Group on International Agricultural Research, "Statistics on Expenditure by International Agricultural Research Centers 1960–1980," World Bank, August 8, 1977.
55. World Health Organization, "A Special Programme for Research and Training in Tropical Diseases," Geneva, September 1975; United Nations Development Programme, Rockefeller Foundation, and World Bank, "Proposal for the Establishment of Cotton Development International," New York, 1977.
56. Carl-Göran Héden, "Microbiological Science for Development: A Global Technological Opportunity," in Ramesh and Weiss, *Mobilizing Technology.*
57. Technological cooperation among developing countries was the topic of a United Nations Conference held in Buenos Aires in September 1978. See, "The Buenos Aires Plan of Action," United Nations Development Programme, New York, 1978, and Enrique Oteiza and Anisur Rahman, "Technical Co-operation Among Third World Countries," Occasional Paper No. 3, Third World Forum, Mexico City, 1978.
58. David Dickson, "Andean Pact Proposes Tax on First World," *Nature,* October 12, 1978.
59. Ariane Van Buren, "Biogas in China," *Ambio,* No. 1, 1980.

Chapter 6: Technical Change and Society

1. Erik Eckholm, *Losing Ground: Environmental Stress and World Food Prospects* (New York: W. W. Norton & Co., 1976).
2. Dorothy Nelkin, *Technological Decisions and Democracy* (London: Sage Publications, 1977).
3. For a review of these agreements, see European Trade Union Institute, *Microelectronics and Employment in the 1980s* (Brussels: 1980).
4. Robert Howard, "Brave New Workplace," *Working Papers,* November/December 1980.
5. British trade union proposals are described by Malcolm Peltu, "In Place of Technological Strife," *New Scientist,* March 13, 1980.
6. For a polemical discussion of some of these points, see Witold Rybczynski, *Paper Heroes* (New York: Anchor Books, 1980).

Index